T D Brown grew up in the North . _ _ugland before going on to study English Literature with Creative Writing at the University of East Anglia.

Tom works as a financial journalist in London.

Dedicated to red wine, insomnia, and long nights without internet.

T D Brown

THE OBLIVIOUS POOL

AUSTIN MACAULEY PUBLISHERS™

LONDON • CAMBRIDGE • NEW YORK • SHARJAH

A CIP catalogue record for this title is available from the British Library.

ISBN 9781398419360 (Paperback)
ISBN 9781398419377 (ePub e-book)

www.austinmacauley.com

First Published 2022
Austin Macauley Publishers Ltd®
1 Canada Square
Canary Wharf
London
E14 5AA

To those without whom this book would not exist, you know who you are.

Cover credit: Niall Brown.

The Dews of Lethe

Smoke tailed from cigarette ends burning in-between parted fingers, wafting up to luggage compartments and mingling amid the briefcases before settling near the electrical light. *Strange*, thought Marshal Sullivan, as he nodded in and out of sleep, to think that the world outside the train flew past at 80 miles per hour, but the smoke still stayed inside.

Someone started speaking in rapid-fire French. Coughing erupted from the back-end of the carriage, waking up Sullivan. The smoke got under his eyelids, stinging the fragile goo inside. He blinked and pushed the jelly back inside his skull with rubbing thumbs, causing lights to dance around the sides of his vision. He sneezed, surprising himself, and took out a handkerchief to blow his nose. It was covered in blood. The marshal frowned, stuffed the garment back into his pocket and wiped his nose on his sleeve, watching for a line of red which did not appear. He checked his holster to feel for his memory cleaner—it was missing.

Right then, a scream echoed around Carriage A, at the same time as the alarm triggered and the backup light failed to switch on, leaving the carriage in darkness. Doors were locked shut, causing the passengers to grumble; a woman at the back was shuddering. Marshal Sullivan rubbed his beard, snorted, spat and ground his teeth before jumping up and striding towards the commotion. He found a frightened woman sat shuddering close to the window, pointing over toward the bathroom where a trickle of red could be followed under the door. Sullivan kicked it open, bursting the lock like an overstretched belt-buckle. The first thing Sullivan noticed about the man was that he was in handcuffs. The next was his eyes; dry porcelain. His chest was a pincushion, tattered bits of cloth black with blood hanging around open wounds. Sullivan crouched down to feel for the pulse, finding none, and went over to the sink to turn off the taps. Water was about to overflow from the sink. He soon spotted blood under the broken fingernails where something had stamped down on them, cracking the delicate pink shells. No accident then.

The woman slipped out of her shoes, still trembling, and headed back to the end of the carriage. He quickly closed the door behind and stepped back out into the dark carriageway.

Ahead of him, he heard angry mutterings, frightened whispers, hushed voices and smelled the early signs of panic.

'A murder,' someone hushed out of the shadows.

'Don't be ridiculous,' scoffed another.

Tutting could be heard from the centre of the carriage.

Someone was still smoking.

'Ladies and gentlemen…' Sullivan flicked off the alarm, switched on the backup lights, then stepped forward before producing his badge. '…Marshal Sullivan speaking, ahem.' He cleared his throat. 'I have been escorting you throughout your journey and need each of you to make your way to the back of the carriage for your own safety. No pushing, please.'

They did as they were told. Sullivan took his time before walking up to the centre of the carriage, allowing his leather shoes to creak on the polished floors as he did so. He took several calculated seconds to look each passenger in the eye before continuing. They were five in total.

He sniffed, 'I need your names, city of residence and citizen IDs. Right away.'

After a few grumbles and a sour expression or two, they all reached down and produced their identification.

'Read them to me,' Sullivan gestured to a man sat on his left, wearing a two-piece tweed suit.

'Sebastian Woolf.' The tweed-wearing man remained seated with his legs raised up on the chair in front. 'London, ID 98442.'

His eyes glinted; his cigarette seemed never to end.

'Michael Cole,' a high-pitched squeak came from behind the dimly lit back-end of the carriage. Two skittish pupils appeared under the lampshades to meet Sullivan's gaze. 'Hull, ID 31270,' the man swallowed, 'I'm the conductor,' he said, sighing as though he were the hostess at a party, embarrassed at her guests arriving early to an untidy home.

'I thought you were the ticket inspector?' asked a perturbed Mr Woolf.

'I'm both,' said the conductor. 'There have been financial setbacks, you see.'

The three men nodded knowingly.

Sullivan's eyes dropped to the well-dressed gentleman in front of him, who stood up and brushed himself down.

'Adrian Nethercott at your service, Marshal,' he removed his bowler hat, uncovering a hairless moor underneath. 'London, 878811. Whatever I can do to help.'

Sullivan nodded and moved on, ignoring the effort Mr Nethercott had made to conceal the pistol holstered behind his right thigh. It was better for the time being, Sullivan decided, to pretend he had not noticed it.

The fourth passenger took some time before replying. She was a skinny woman with wide hips who had been busy filing her nails without raising her head which was hidden underneath a large crimson hat. Sullivan recognised her as the one who had discovered the blood; her demeanour had changed as quickly as her shoes. But trauma could do funny things to a person, he knew better than most.

'Ah…' her eyes jumped up to the rest of the group. 'Elisabeth Collett, a pleasure to meet you all,' she tipped her sun hat in their direction, smiling pleasantly at everyone. 'Paris, as you like, Marshal. Visitor number 0056.'

Mr Nethercott bolted upright in his chair and said,

'What's a Frenchwoman doing in England?'

Miss Collett pointed her well-shaped eyebrows in his direction.

'Why, whatsoever she pleases, I should imagine. The war is over, no?'

Sullivan silenced Mr Nethercott by clearing his throat again and waving a hand. He walked over to the man on his right, the only one to have remained silent throughout the journey so far.

'And you, citizen?'

The man didn't reply. He was staring at his knees with a vacant expression as though half asleep. His ID was poking out from his coat pocket as though he had been expecting the request. Sullivan plucked it from him and began to read aloud:

'Jack Jackson, Manchester—16188.' Sullivan raised an eyebrow a fraction and said,

'Your name is Jack Jackson?'

'Yes, sir.'

Jack Jackson didn't look up.

Sullivan curled a lip. 'Didn't have a very creative father?'

'Yes, sir.'

Sullivan snorted.

'Very well.' He turned back to the party and addressed them from the front of the carriage. 'Ladies and gentleman, I regret to inform you all that there has been a death aboard this train. It is my duty, as a Marshal of the law, to place this carriage on lockdown, for the safety of the other passengers on board this train, until such time as my investigation is completed. I shall need you all to submit to a memory inspection of the last hour, at which point this train departed from Manchester.'

Shocked expressions greeted his announcement. Mr Woolf's arms refolded. Mr Nethercott's knuckles were cracked and Miss Collett's nail-file stopped seesawing at the end of her fingers and clattered to the floor.

'Come off it, Marshal,' snorted Mr Woolf, 'We weren't the only ones to talk to the inventor. We're wasting time while the culprit has likely gotten away already.'

Sullivan adjusted his cuffs while watching the others for reactions, but inside he was calculating. An inventor? The dead man was known already, it seemed.

'May I remind you all,' he took a moment to choose his words, 'that at a crime scene, an officer has the right to stop and search any citizen within sight and to ask them to submit to a memory inspection on the spot. You five are the only passengers who had access to the bathroom, it follows that only one of those present can be responsible for the murder. Consider it one of the trade-offs of traveling first class.'

'This—' Mr Nethercott stammered with indolence, 'this is preposterous. You cannot mean to say we are all suspects?'

Sullivan opened his mouth to reply but was beaten to the mark.

'That's exactly what he is saying, my good man,' Mr Woolf smiled at him. 'Nowadays we're all guilty until proven innocent,' he added.

Sullivan frowned, clearing his throat to regain their attention, and started unfastening memory uploaders from his belt. He walked to stand over Mr Woolf, who raised his head to frown at the Marshal, as one might at an insect about to be splattered.

'I think we will start with you first,' said Sullivan, offering him a memory uploader.

The lamp swayed from side to side as the train bumped over a ridge in the tracks, and the light was thrown from one corner to the other. When it had settled, Mr Woolf had a big smile plastered over his lips. He was chuckling.

'Marshal,' Mr Nethercott approached him from the side, the skinny man bending nervously, 'if we might speak privately a moment...'

'We can speak privately,' said Sullivan, advancing another step towards the seated businessman, 'once Mr Woolf has undergone his memory inspection.'

Mr Nethercott persisted, forehead polished with sweat, 'I, I really think it's important that we speak alone—'

'You heard the man, Marshal,' Mr Woolf used the opportunity to ease even deeper into his chair, a barricade of folded arms in front. 'He wants to speak in private. A confession, perhaps? You're doing yourself a disservice by standing here another minute without hearing what the fellow has to say.'

Sullivan's hand swept down past his belt and drew his blazer away from his torso, brushing past his pistol holstered to his left hip, and up to the handcuffs hidden by his blazer.

'I'll go first.' A timid voice from the back of the room turned every head present. It was the conductor, still cowering behind the lampshade. 'I was the one who tripped the alarm. I found the body. I should go first,' he said, his voice drained of all enthusiasm for the task. 'You need to see what I saw, Marshal.' He crept forward, walking on ice without skates, and reached towards Sullivan's outstretched hand to pick an uploader from his grip.

The conductor winced as he took the uploader and twisted the metal into the back of his head, screwing it with well-practiced hands. His eyes rolled in their sockets. Limbs shuddered, teeth chattered, neuron patterns were mapped out on to infinitesimal slithers of metal, and after a minute the uploader was ready for collection.

Sullivan, approaching the man, unscrewed the uploader containing the fresh memory and twisted it straight into his own head. The others were staring at the Marshal, his spine tingling as the metal bit into the bone, getting used to the weight of the uploader in his skull. He felt the new memories begin to itch at the base of his neck, taking hold of his innermost thoughts. He sat down on the nearest chair, pressed the trigger and began to upload them. His fingers and toes started to twitch and dance and quiver, and then dance some more, until the memories overcame him.

***

'Five minutes, miss. If I haven't seen your ticket by then, I'm afraid you'll have to get off at the next stop.'

The woman sat upright in haughty defiance crimson hat casting her face in shadow. She stuffed a letter back inside her handbag and glared at him, pale as powder.

She muttered something in French under her breath.

'Okay?' said Michael, eyeing her before turning around and striding off to the end of the carriage. He made a show of checking the last few tickets at a leisurely pace, edging away from her vicinity, just to make sure she got the message.

She was a looker. Pale skin, dark eyes, expensive-looking hair. Classy, but in a loose, self-contemptuous sort of way. He imagined, as he often did with the women he spoke to on-board, what it would be like to have sex with her; whether her pinned-back hair would stay in place or not. He would have liked to find a way to direct her with a warm smile and a soft voice, but there was no way around it. You give them an inch, they take a mile.

He reached the end of the carriageway and realised he had nothing to do there except walk back to the front of the carriage. He decided to hang back a bit and examine his ticket puncher, assuring that anyone glancing his way would see a train conductor hard at work. He checked his watch…three minutes. Well, if she didn't have it by now, he doubted another minute or two would make a difference.

He grinned and began to shuffle his way back down the aisle. Before he left, he heard grunting coming from inside the bathroom. A musky sighing, followed by a squelching noise, which could be heard even over the sound of the train wheels. He put his ear to the door and made out two distinct voices.

Good grief, he thought, unable to believe his own ears. Of all the unruly acts he'd been forced to deal with in his time training to be a conductor, this one took the cake. Surely there were more discreet places for buggery than a train bathroom? Dear oh dear. He shook his head, deciding to deal with this in the most direct manner. He hammered on the door.

'Oy,' he said, in what he hoped was a stern voice, 'I can hear you in there—stop it this instant. I'm giving you three seconds to open this door.'

Three seconds passed, but no reply came.

Michael dithered, unsure what to do next.

'Right,' he said, at last, 'if that's the way it's going to be, I'm coming in there. I'm giving you one more chance.'

Nothing happened.

He wheeled around and marched off back to the conductor's carriage, keenly aware that he had no way of entering the bathroom if it was locked from the inside. He fumbled around the control room, trying to think of what should be done. He could hardly wait outside during the entire train journey. Besides, what was he going to do with them when he caught them?

He ransacked the conductor's drawer and grasped a screwdriver, thinking he might be able to unscrew the lock if they refused to come out. The train rumbled over a bridge and the countryside opened up out of the window as Michael ambled down to the bathroom again, forgetting all about the lady at the back. He walked past a tweed-dressed man reading the newspaper and a man in uniform who was fast asleep.

He gently unscrewed the bolts on the lock, taking care to be quiet so he would have the element of surprise on his side.

He shook his head again. What on earth he was going to do if it was two gentlemen in there, he had no idea.

The final bolt fell and the door creaked open with tentative ease.

'Alright,' he said, 'I'm coming in.'

He pushed the door and felt it slam into something with a thunk, jamming the entrance. Michael frowned, leaning his weight into it, but the door was stopped again by something soft on the other side.

'Hey,' said Michael, angry now. He tried to wriggle into the bathroom by sliding a leg through the crack and wedging himself through. 'You're in big trouble if—'

His foot landed in something wet.

He gasped, off balance, and stumbled into the room, both shoes squelching as they planted themselves inside. Had the sink been blocked? The toilet? His fumbling hand found the light switch, and a pathetic whimper escaped his lips, drowned out by the engine in the carriageway... but in the bathroom it echoed as loud as any scream. The first thing he saw the dead man's face. His fiery, ginger hair was soggy with blood, soaking it up like a mop with no bucket. One leg was twisted up against the door from when Michael had slammed into it, with the corpse's arms wrapped around itself, as though embarrassed to show the tattered streaks of cloth the knife had left behind. As Michael recoiled, he caught a view of glistening intestines, slipping over the man's fingers in ropey ribbons where he had tried to stuff them back into himself. Michael's legs were suddenly made of hot jelly and his mouth had gone dry. He had to get out, to get away; to get anywhere.

He slithered back through the opening, one toe at a time, hovering a few inches above a pool of blood-curdled water. Before the final inch of him had escaped, he caught a glimpse of the pale dead face, staring at the wall opposite with eyes askew, and realised with horror that the face was a familiar one. Hadn't he seen that shaggy ginger mane only this morning in the paper? Could it be the inventor? No, no, he was supposed to be in London. His mind must be traumatised, playing tricks.

Michael scarpered away and closed the bathroom door shut, sweat running down his forehead. There was only one thing to be done. Without thinking twice, he carried on down the carriageway, leaving bloody footprints behind him leading to the conductor's carriage. That was when he hit the emergency switch and placed all the carriages on lockdown, sealing the passengers inside.

Right before the light went out, he saw someone get up to use the bathroom and heard a woman's scream. Chaos erupted, and a few moments later someone with a police badge was stood up and shouting orders. He shuffled to the back of the room along with everyone else.

***

When Sullivan came back to being himself, the lighting had changed. It took a while for the people around him to come back into focus, his mind still busy shaking off the old memories. He looked down at his hands, seeing the smooth pink fingers of Mr Cole replaced by his own gnarled, knobbly workman's hands. He rubbed them together and then raised them to his nose, basking in their scent before looking around the room. Smell was a powerful anchor.

Mr Woolf was redoing his tie into an elegant double-Windsor knot, while Mr Nethercott was pacing up and down, looking anywhere except the end of the hall where the body lay encased inside its bathroom coffin and Miss Collett busied herself perusing her handbag, a taut frown creasing her powdered forehead. Mr Cole was slumped back into a chair, staring out of the window with his feet hooked behind the chair legs underneath.

Sullivan went straight up to the conductor, who jolted upright as the Marshal approached.

'A word?' he asked, and beckoned the man to the back of the carriage so that they might talk unheard. They went inside the conductor's carriage and sealed the door.

'Was it me?' Mr Cole squeaked as soon as they were out of earshot, 'I don't remember it, sir, I swear. I know that's what they all say but…'

'What?' asked Sullivan, fluttering his eyes against the light, 'No, of course not.'

'Oh,' said Mr Cole, deflating like a punctured balloon, 'sorry, I thought somehow…never mind.' Mr Cole looked desperately at the floor while Sullivan stared at him.

'The train,' Sullivan gestured at the controls, 'can't you stop it? The emergency power seems to have set us on a direct course for London.'

'Nothing I can do, sir,' the young lad shook his head. He must have been about 25, 23? 'First week on the job, they never showed me how to override the autopilot.'

'And the radio? Can you not radio for help?'

'It was out of order when I started, sir.'

Sullivan sighed.

The victim, you know why he was in handcuffs, don't you?'

The young lad hesitated, his Adam's apple quivering as his mouth parted to speak

He pressed the boy. You recognised him as an inventor, but did not know the name?'You could not remember at the time. Have you remembered it since?'

'I have,' nodded the conductor, eyes bright with the prospect of being helpful. 'Callum McClean, Scottish inventor, to be tried for murder.'

The train rattled and Sullivan caught the lamp above to stop it from swinging, pointing it straight into Mr Cole's eyes.

'For murder? You mean to tell me the man is to be tried for a crime?'

'Well, he was,' Mr Cole corrected him. 'Suppose there wouldn't be much use in it now, seeing that he's dead.'

'What was he doing here?'

'That I cannot tell you, sir. I saw him sitting, but because of his long hair I couldn't see his face.'

Sullivan paused to think. His memory was hazy, slow and clouded with fog. Now that he came to think of it, he was having a little trouble remembering what had been happening before he fell asleep. 'Whom did he murder?'

'Another inventor, sir, named Mr Bell.'

'He and this Mr Bell, they knew each other?'

'Acquaintances I believe. They were both working on the same project; full memory transfer, the papers were calling it. It would have let someone completely transfer their entire memory, childhood memory and all sir, though I don't rightly know who'd be volunteering for that one. Mr Bell claimed to have first invented and filed a patent. McClean went berserk, said that Mr Bell stole his design, and murdered the man in his home, so they say. He was to swing in London, all the papers said so. Didn't you read it, sir?'

'No, I'm afraid I've been a little behind on the news of late.'

Mr Cole took a glance at the dim, cavernous bathroom at the end of the carriageway, then back to Sullivan. 'I daresay you might be caught up real soon, sir.'

***

The two of them returned to find that Mr Woolf had lit a cigarette in their absence.

'Caught him then, have you?' he asked, nodding towards Mr Cole. 'That was quick. But then things are often found in the first place we look.'

Sullivan ignored his comment, darting forwards and offering an uploader in his outstretched hand. 'We can do it this way,' he said in a hushed voice, 'or in handcuffs. It's your choice.'

The businessman shrugged, leaning back into a have-it-your-way slouch, twisting the uploader into the back of his head and passing it back to Sullivan once he was done.

Sullivan resumed his previous sitting position after screwing in the new memories. His fingers began to tremble.

***

It was a chilly September morning, and Sebastian had been debating with himself for some time as to whether he

22

should bark at a passing waiter to pump some more hot water into the pipes from the boiler before he caught a chill, or go to the trouble of pulling his coat closer around him before his meal arrived. To warm himself further, Sebastian had fashioned a cocoon of about six different newspapers, four telegrams and a dozen letters spread over every bit of the available table space, which in first class, was considerable.

Woolf & Co. was the leading world supplier of steel, and Sebastian intended to keep it that way. He did this by operating a strict reading-schedule, updating his knowledge of the related markets every time he found himself traveling. He traced the price of steel over the course of six weeks, then compared it with the price of pig iron. Gold had spiked after negotiations to start mines in the Ashanti Empire had failed, leaving the treasures potentially buried there forever. The price of silver had fallen off a cliff after the Germans stopped minting the coins last Christmas, but so far iron had stayed afloat. Since then, Woolf & Co.'s exports to the American colonies had increased by thirty percent, and they were currently in talks with a partner company to expand into the Caribbean as well. They were waiting for official protection from the crown to guarantee them safe passage—but Her Majesty was in no mood to make promises so soon after the war.

He wrote down the figures from the New York Stock Exchange and then cross-referenced them with London's own figures. There had been a market shudder yesterday, and traders were being cautious. Austria's economy had taken a beating after the demonetisation of silver. He had taken several trips to Frankfurt and Vienna not too long ago, and several lawyers he trusted had assured him that the bumps were temporary and they expected the economy to be back on track very soon. The stock of Cooke & Company, Woolf & Co.'s biggest rival, had fallen over 6% according to this morning's report. That made him smile, but he could not afford to be careless. He put a big circle around India and jotted down a note to remind him to write a letter to the East India Company later in the evening. He had tried to arrange a meeting with Mr Clive's secretary several times, but their calendars never seemed to match up.

He scanned the headlines notepad at the ready.

Sabastian took a red pen to the words"equine outbreaks" and "dying down".

They entered a tunnel, throwing the notes into darkness. Sebastian saw only the outlines of bold lettering, trying to guess at their contents. He saw more headlines and began circling Rumours of "South American governments in renewed talks" a—a-hah! They exited the runnel, with the news story gleaming bright in front of him. He made a mental note to send a few telegrams to the South American Union once they got to London Steel would continue to rise, after all.

Sunrays darted in and out of the carriage windows as the train emerged from the tunnel, bouncing off the waitress' gleaming smile as she flew a plate of steaming boar-ribs down to land on Sebastian's table. He thanked her with a tilt of the head and a courteous wink. She blushed, smiling again, the light bouncing off her bulletproof teeth, and left the sizzling food in front of him. He held her gaze as she turned away and walked back down the carriageway, his eyes doing the smiling for him. Carriage A was filled with the type of cheap, grey fog that only cigarettes can produce. The smoke mixed with the condensation wafting from the food, carrying up his nostrils in a delightful mix of smells that was equal parts burnt tar, overdone sirloin and roasted vegetables. Perfection.

He had written a letter this morning to his brother-in-law who had invited him out to go star-gazing out in his country house when he arrived in London:

Thank you for your invitation in your last letter, brother, but I fear you must have mistaken me for someone else, he had written. *In the evenings, I do not read, I do not play cards, I do not go stargazing. My only pleasure is my business.*

He had been harsh, he knew. Perhaps he should have softened his tone, but such hindsight did not serve a man well. One day, perhaps when he was retired, he would have time to go star-gazing. He had always been interested in astronomy, and he would often spend many hours alone at night, with only himself and the night sky for company. Maybe in another life he could have been a pioneer of such sort, one who could taste every flavour of life before his short years were over. But time, time! It is the only thing in the world we can't get more of.

But despite all that, a fine meal on board a train was one thing he could rely on. He grabbed hold of his knife and fork and was about to tuck-in when the ticket inspector arrived. He had already been through one time, and in Mr Woolf's experience, there was never a good reason to see a ticket inspector twice.

'Excuse me, sir,' said the boy, maybe a little older than his own son would have been.

Sebastian sighed and pushed his plate to the far side of the table.

'Excuse me, sir, but there's been a mix up with the seating. I'm afraid—'

'No.'

'Sir?'

'I do not think I will excuse you. Why are you interrupting my meal?'

There was a pointed pause.

Sebastian rolled his shoulders back, enjoying the tension. 'Well?'

'As I said, sir, there's been a mix up with the seating. Seat 7B is reserved for the police sergeant who just joined us at the last stop.'

He gestured toward a man who had been lurking behind him who suddenly stepped forwards. He was a skinny man, wearing a bowler hat with enough tilt to give the illusion of hair underneath. He had a pistol at his side and a badge on his front.

Sergeant Nethercott, it read.

'Sorry, old chap,' the sergeant tipped his hat at him. 'Hate to be rude, hate to be rude. State business you see.'

Sebastian eyed the London bobby and folded his paper. He thought about making a scene, of asking the do-you-know-who-I-am question, of perhaps alerting the other passengers on the train to the injustice taking place. But would they care? He very much doubted it. Embarrassing the official would be to no one's benefit.

'Please,' he said, swooping out of the way while gesturing towards the empty chair, 'I've been keeping it warm for you.'

The waiter took his food and followed Sebastian away from the table. He located a spot four seats behind but in the same carriage and asked the waiter to put the plate down. He sat behind two empty seats so he could watch the bobby.

As soon as he started eating again, he saw the Londoner disappear. He soon returned with a large, hulking figure sporting a ginger mane and arms bigger than the slimmer man's torso. The big man growled and Sebastian caught a distinctive Scottish twang.

'This way, McClean,' muttered the smaller man to the larger, and plonked him down on the window side. He had a shaggy mane of red hair which covered his face. He did not look up or speak, but his figure towered over the rest of the passengers.

Sebastian caught a flash of silver before he was hidden from view.

The Scotsman was in handcuffs. Interesting.

The next hour or so passed without incident, and Sebastian proceeded to eat his meal in peace. Once he had finished, he decided to read the Sunday paper which had been left on his new seat. The headline read:

'Memory transfer' plans stolen by foreign spy in Manchester

Tabloid nonsense, surmised Sebastian, who proceeded to look out of the window. Soon bored, he picked up the paper and began reading. He was flabbergasted once he read that the new memory transfer technology was suspected to have been stolen by the French government. Why, they had only just finished giving the bastards a licking at the Rhine, now they had the gall to undercut a revolutionary technology? The audacity was overbearing.

The agents, he read, had waited until the patent had been filled, and then broken into the patent office to steal the prototype and transfer it onto a memory uploader. The culprits had yet to be caught, running off with the uploader and hiding it, but they believed an officer had switched sides and was working for the French. He read about the murdered inventor, to be put on trial in London. A Scotsman? With a police escort? Sebastian looked up at the pair who had taken his seat and put two and two together.

He looked back to the finance section and read that memory stock was trading at 0.8 points down from yesterday, sinking the value.

The Scotsman was getting up, with the sergeant pointing in the direction of the bathroom. Sebastian watched from over the top of the paper until he was out of sight, then buried his nose back inside its paper fortress

He made a mental note to ask his secretary to keep an eye on French investment in memory-transfer tech. Sebastian was never one to miss out on an opportunity. He had contacts in Paris; he would make a few calls on Monday.

He read the name of the lead suspect printed in bold under a warning that the turncoat office was not to be approached.

Patrick Blake, it read.

Just at that moment, a scream echoed throughout the carriage. Then the lights all went off at once and flickered back into life a minute later. Sebastian whirled around just in time to see a greying Marshal standing atop a table, holding his badge. There was a pool of blood behind him near the bathrooms.

'Excuse me, ladies and gentlemen, Marshal Sullivan speaking…'

***

Images swam in and out of focus. The room reoriented itself from the screaming, bloody mess of half an hour ago, and back into the orderly line of passengers sitting in front of him. Sullivan blinked four times, pumping the blood through his arms by rubbing them until the feeling came back and he was sure he was in his own body again. He was uploading too fast, he thought. It was taking longer to revert each time.

'So?' asked an impatient Mr Woolf, 'Am I the murderer?'

Sullivan straightened his jacket, sniffed and pointed at Mr Nethercott while glaring at the businessman. 'You knew about this? You knew and said nothing?'

Mr Woolf twiddled the ends of his moustache and raised an eyebrow. 'You did not ask,' was all he said.

'I believe I can explain, Marshal,' said Mr Nethercott, throwing out a hand to stop Sullivan from advancing on the seated man further. 'If you could give me a moment to explain…'

'You'll have to forgive my aversion to unwanted surprises, Sergeant Nethercott,' Sullivan removed his hat, black bristles brushing against the fabric. 'I did not realise we had a fellow officer on board.'

Mr Nethercott blanched. 'You seemed to have the situation quite under control, Marshal; I had no wish to derail your investigation.' He gestured at the rest of the group, who looked ill at ease at the revelation of yet another law official in their midst. That is, everyone bar Mr Woolf, who beamed as though being temporarily cleared of murder had placed him in a vastly superior social category.

Mr Nethercott went on, 'My mission was intended to be, ah, a little more discreet shall we say.'

'If you don't mind my asking, Sergeant…' began Sullivan as the sergeant balanced on the balls of his feet, 'Was the deception really necessary?'

The man bristled. 'Why, we had only departed the station a moment earlier when cries of bloody murder were in the air. Can you forgive me for being too cautious?'

Sullivan supposed that he could. He looked at the rest of the group, who had discovered the tea trolley, and were busy making themselves a brew while they waited.

'Sergeant, may we speak a moment?' he paused. 'In private?'

Sullivan led them both towards the back of the carriage where the loose curtains of the conductor's carriage shielded them from view. Mr Nethercott took out a pipe and began loading it with tobacco.

'You must understand my caution, Marshal,' muttered the Sergeant, who located a matchbox in his trouser pocket and set an orange orb glowing at the end of his pipe. 'This has far greater implications than a mere professional rivalry that got out of hand…It involves our new so-called "allies", the Prussians and the French, who were funding my prisoner's prototype. I believe we have a spy on board.'

'A spy?' Sullivan raised an eyebrow.

'Yes, a foreign agent if you will.'

'In all honesty, I am beginning to have serious doubts the killer did not escape the moment the deed was done,' continued Sullivan.

'I have no doubt in your abilities, Marshal,' said the sergeant between puffs. 'We will find out who did this, I promise you. But first, we need to consider that this was a planned attack by another power.'

Sullivan coughed as he inhaled second-hand fumes and waved the smoke away.

'This prisoner of yours…' began Sullivan, as his companion apologised for the smoke, 'You say he was an inventor? Being funded by the French?'

'Correct, Marshal,' Mr Nethercott let a bellow of smoke escape from the corners of his mouth. 'He was competing with his contemporary, Alexander Bell, whose petition for funding was rejected by the French government. The two were racing to be the first to facilitate a full-memory transfer. Can you imagine such a thing, Marshal? The ability to transfer one's entire consciousness to another host, instead of just the fragments we share with each other every day? McClean claims that he was the original inventor, but we have the patent submission to disprove him. Jealousy can be a dangerous beast.' He shook his head, exasperated. 'I knew letting him out of sight to use the bathroom was a terrible idea. But once I had him on the train, I suspected no foul play.'

He set into a series of coughs which Sullivan took no notice of, he was too busy thinking. *Why would the French fund a memory-transfer developer right on the brink of the war's end? What could they hope to gain?*

'And the prototype,' the Marshal continued once Mr Nethercott had regained his breath, 'what became of it?'

'Stolen just last night,' he sent a smoke ring to envelope the nearest light-bulb. 'A perpetrator with the help of one of our own officers. Patrick Blake, I believe his name was.' Mr Nethercott looked taken aback when Sullivan failed to react.

'I'm familiar with the name,' he told the Sergeant, 'I read it in the paper.'

***

They emerged to join with the others. All of them were in the thick of conversation as they approached. Mr Woolf had begun talking to Mr Cole, who sat as still as the furniture while the two officers approached. Sullivan noticed Jack Jackson, however, who had been sat completely oblivious to the rest of the party for some time. His eyes were still averted, and Sullivan had his suspicions that the man was simple or perhaps a deaf-mute, for he seemed unable to comprehend those who spoke to him.

'Can you hear me, friend?'

Everyone turned their head to look at Jack Jackson, as though only just now realising he existed. Sullivan walked up to the table to where the uploaders were laying, humming like overworked light-bulbs. He picked up the one for Jack Jackson and proceeded to screw it into the port at the back of his skull. The man did not react, merely gritting his teeth as the download trigger was pulled, and then once again was still. Sullivan retracted the uploader after unscrewing it gently, expecting the man to lash out or protest, but he did nothing. Sullivan raised the slither of metal, and dived into the darkness once again.

***

Still, eerie blackness swirled around him in invisible circles. His body parts were beginning to evaporate. He tried to scream and could not. He tried to breathe and could not. He was coalescing into a gaseous form, his hands, feet, eyes, ears and nose, detaching like leaves from a tree and blowing downwind. The urge to think, to exist, had left him, and one-by-one his last remaining inklings of consciousness began to slip away. He imagined, if imagining was what it was, that he would exist this way forever. It reminded him of standing in the shower before he went to work. He would stand, his feet glued to the ground, rolling his shoulders and staring at the floor. He would think about pleasant things, like what it had been like to go fishing with his father, or stealing cakes from the school cafeteria. He would smile and stare at the water trickling down the drain—knowing that any moment now he would have to turn the shower off and step out of the warmth, back into the real world. But even those memories were beginning to detach and drift away from him, as though they belonged to a stranger living in some place very far away.

'Marshal?'

Hands appeared out of the blackness, shaking what was left of his corporeal form.

'Marshal, snap out of it!'

A splash of cold water brought him crashing back to reality. He sputtered, swinging his fists on instinct. There was a gasp as his knuckles skimmed something. He rolled over, something sharp was poking him in the back, and why was he lying on the floor?

'What…'

Light shot into the back of his retinas as his eyes snapped open, immobilising him. He began to see three figures unblurring themselves above. Miss Collet, Mr Nethercott and Mr Woolf; their faces furrowed into ridges of concern.

Miss Collett offered him a timid hand; her grip strong enough to make him fear for his fingers.

He stood up, wobbling. 'How long was I…?'

She steadied him. 'A matter of minutes,' she almost looked embarrassed for him.

'Minutes?' he shook his head. It had felt like hours. His clammy hands looked gaunt and drained of blood. He clasped them together to stop them from shaking and began to rub his arms and legs once they were rested. Finally, he massaged his temples until the blood returned to his scalp and he could be sure his thoughts were his own. He had only ever had one similar experience throughout his career, but it was a sensation impossible to mistake.

His nose was running so he took out his handkerchief to blow it. Sullivan saw once again, but only just now remembered, that it was covered in blood, ruining the white embroidering. Did he have a nose bleed? He quickly stuffed it out of sight before anyone saw, and the memory of it soon slipped away from him.

He walked over to Jack Jackson as soon as he was able. Jackson had not made a move throughout the unfolding drama. Sullivan immediately took out a match and began holding it up to his pupils. Although they dilated, he refrained from blinking.

'Very susceptible,' Sullivan muttered to himself, blowing out the match. 'Stand up please, Mr Jackson.'

Jack Jackson did as he was commanded.

'Now sit back down.'

He followed suit.

'Good, thank you.' He reached out with his thumb and forefinger and, with a pincer-grip, pinched Jack Jackson's right ear and twisted.

A gasp of sympathy echoed around the carriage from Miss Collett's corner, but apart from a slight jerk of the head, Jack Jackson gave no sign that he had felt any pain.

'Just as I thought,' announced the Marshal, 'a clean wipe. He doesn't even have residual memory left. Lucky, considering what might have happened to him in Manchester, if he'd been found in this state.'

The Marshal shuddered at the memory of that horrid emptiness. If he went the rest of his life without living through that again he would not die unhappy.

'A casual vagabond,' remarked Mr Nethercott, hovering around the two of them and gesturing gratuitously. 'From the workhouses, I'll bet my watch. No doubt he sold every slither of memory he had for a train ticket and an ounce of opium, planning to pick up some handout-memory once he arrives in the capital.' He rummaged in his coat pocket. 'Well, I'll be damned if I'll have another street urchin accosting the locals outside the station.' He quickly brought out an ink-coated badge and stamped two black marks on each of Mr Jackson's hands.

VAGRANT, the bold letters declared, **DO NOT ASSIST**.

'What's wrong with him?' asked Miss Collett, looking aghast as Jack Jackson lifted his hands away to gaze at them with misty goldfish-eyes.

'He's been negged,' said Sullivan without turning around, 'sold his memory away, or had it sold, probably right before he boarded, from the look of him. Bought a ticket with the proceeds and slept in the station to avoid going through security; only soon after you forget why you were in the station in the first place. Poor bugger doesn't even have childhood memories left. You lose all your foundation, who you are, what you want for yourself, but it's one way to get out of the workhouses.'

Miss Collett looked at the man as though he were centre stage of some grotesque circus show of which Sullivan was the ringmaster.

'He did this to himself?' her throat closed on the last word.

'Most likely,' Sullivan's head started moving in a rhythmic nod as he explained, 'He looks like a warehouse worker to me, they're usually the type. Sometimes it's beggars.' He thought about telling her about the opium habits that were often sustained through selling off one fragmented memory at a time, often weeding out every positive memory they had until the only ones left were those of decrepit, stinking, torturous misery that the black market had no use for. That was when the opium would run out, and the oblivious pool was the only option. They would go to the black-market traffickers to plunge themselves into the dark waters of the Lethe—drink deep, and have all memories of their past lives obliterated, hoping to be born again on the back of state welfare. He kept those insights to himself, though. 'He'll be picked up by the bobbies along the way, no point troubling him now.'

Mr Woolf shuddered and obscured the sight of the man with a newspaper as Sullivan turned away from the invalid. He stood up; there was a murder still to be solved.

'And who buys this memory?' asked Miss Collett, who, unlike anyone else, did not seem to want to let the subject drop. 'Other criminals?'

Sullivan shrugged. 'Sometimes, if the memory is useful; like fighting or pick-pocketing, but most of the time it's ordinary folk...parents buying language memory to get their kids into school early, you know. People buy what they can afford. And as long as it's cheap, they don't ask questions about where it came from.'

While Sullivan was going through the man's pockets, he found a small, expensive-looking case and popped it open without letting the others see. Inside was a diamond ring with a velvet cushion holding it in place. He sighed to himself, realising the poor lad had likely found a lady down in the big city and bitten off more than he could chew on the memory-market in his hurry to ask for her hand in marriage. He thought about confiscating it, then scolded himself, and put it back in the man's pocket. Maybe whoever he was looking for would find him one day.

The Frenchwoman had watery eyes when Sullivan approached her table to hand her an uploader.

'Will that happen to me?' she asked him in a low voice so the others couldn't hear. 'If I'm cornered and alone in an alleyway in this country, will that happen to me?'

Sullivan paused with the uploader in hand, eyeing her and seeing the same fear he once felt when seeing a negging for the first time.

'No,' he said, quietly, so the sound would not reach the others. 'Not while I'm here.' He held her gaze for just a brief second, pushing back against a wall of thoughts and feelings that came from him or one of the many other consciousnesses he had inhabited this morning. Suddenly, the train shot through a tunnel, and for a moment the carriage seemed to drift as it passed through the darkness, floating above solid ground, as though it were being ferried from one shore to the next, and then the moment passed.

When the light returned, she was seated, with her memories already prepared for him to extract. Sullivan screwed the uploader inside his head and veered off out of view to peruse the memories in private, lest any of their contents overwhelm him again. He hid himself in the bathroom, stepping over the handcuffed body, and let the thoughts envelop him alone.

***

The train engine huffed and puffed over the sound of clinking cutlery. It was clear she was on a train at least, but why? She spun her head over her shoulder and swivelled it from left to right, trying to catch a familiar face. There were none.

It occurred to Elisabeth that she had no idea who she was or where she was going. *How strange*, she thought, immediately thinking it odd that she would wake up on a train without having a handler with her.

There were small mutterings around her. A second's worth of concentration told her that no one was speaking French. Were they in Prussia? The Gozitan Nation?

She heard the waiter talking to a man in a tweed suit at the back of the carriage, who began to chuckle and reply in accented English.

Ah. She was in Britain then.

Elisabeth tried to remember the last time she had dreamt, and what language it had been in. She could not.

How long had she been in this part of the world? Where were her children?

She focused on the waiter's conversation with the businessman.

'Are you all alright, sir?'

'Alright? Why shouldn't I be?'

'Well, you looked as though you might be bothered by something. I was wondering if there was anything I could do for you.'

'Tell me, my good man, do you know how many stars are there in the sky?

'Why, I'm sure I couldn't tell you without looking at them, sir.'

'Indeed. How long do you think it would take you to lay down in a field, and count every single one?'

'I don't know, sir?'

'Too much time, my good fellow. Far too much time. Time is the only thing we don't have in abundance, you know, in the modern world.'

He got back to his newspaper and the waiter disappeared. Miss Collett returned to her seat and looked around for her handbag, confused. She soon discovered that she was being watched. The train conductor had caught her eye and was loitering around the back of the train. He was moving down the middle, inspecting each passenger's ticket.

'Tickets please,' came the ringing decree over the noise of the rolling carriage wheels.

Elisabeth probed the depths of her handbag, but could not find her ticket. Instead, they closed around a letter. She pulled it out and held it up in a tentative grip. It was addressed to her. On the front, someone had written in scribbled handwriting:

OPEN IN LONDON

She glanced around at the other passengers to see if anyone was looking at her. When she decided they were not, she tore open the letter and began to read:

Dear Elisabeth,

If you are reading this and are not in police custody, you have arrived in London. Hopefully, you will have forgotten all about me. I need to stress that it is necessary, absolutely necessary, that you do not read this letter until you are off the train; for my safety, and more importantly, your own. We have been separated, but we will be together again soon, my love. In order for this to happen, however, you must do exactly as instructed. By now, as you will no doubt be aware—

'Tickets please,' a droning voice tore her eyes away from the letter. The ticket inspector, a young boy, was standing over her wielding a ticket puncher in one hand and a notepad in the other. 'Tickets, madam.'

'Oh, sorry,' she stuffed the letter down to her feet and resumed her ransack of the handbag. The ticket inspector waited impatiently. 'I know it's here somewhere…' she wilted with embarrassment. 'I'm very sorry, sir, I can show it to you in one moment?'

The ticket inspector harrumphed, eyebrows receding up almost as far as his hairline. 'I must see it before we arrive in Birmingham, or you will be asked to leave the train.'

Her eyes begged for mercy. 'But I'm sure I have misplaced it. I have the receipt, look.'

He ignored her.

'Ten minutes, miss. If I haven't seen your ticket by then, I'm afraid you'll have to get off at the next stop.'

Elisabeth hid the letter.

'Wet chicken,' she muttered below hearing volume.

'Okay?' he said, and walked away.

Elisabeth slumped back in her chair, bewildered. Where had she put it? She gave one last hurried search but was forced to give up. It was nowhere to be found. The conductor would throw her off the train at Birmingham, and then she didn't know what she was going to do. While searching, she found the strange letter she had discovered in her handbag, now crumpled up, and began to read again:

...As you will no doubt be aware, the inventor has been murdered and his plans stolen. They have been destroyed, but committed to memory; a memory we will uncover in Paris together. If everything has gone according to plan, you will have been questioned by the police and released, while the suspect will be behind bars awaiting execution. But the real murderer, I, who have written this confession, will soon be by your side. You have no memory of this, or of me, because I have wiped both of our memories to protect you. You will know how to find me after you are out of danger, and find me

you must, for as long as we are separated, I shall forever be miserable.

Your friend and lover,
Patrick Blake

***

Sullivan arrived back into reality with a shake of the head and a splash of water to scare away the false memories. He looked at his gaunt features in the mirror. Dark ringed eyes gazed back at him—bloodshot from memory visions—veins pulsing in his neck as his mouth twisted into a grimace. The name written on Miss Collett's letter flashed at him without warning as the memories began to fade.

PATRICK BLAKE

He looked around for tissues and remembered he had a handkerchief in his pocket. He fumbled inside, reaching for it, and felt something wet. He withdrew the handkerchief, embroidered with that white, pearly thread. It was covered in blood.

Sullivan dropped it in shock and slammed up against the wall, as though seeing it for the first time. He had picked it up two times before, but he had forgotten it. Was something blocking his long-term memory? He remembered his memory cleaner, and checked for it in his holster, realising for the second time that day that it was missing. What had happened to it? What, precisely, had he been doing before falling asleep on board the train?

42

Thinking now, exactly when he had gotten aboard the train? Was it at Manchester? At what time? What did the station look like? He could not remember.

He reached down to pick up the handkerchief, and as his fingers brushed it, something in his coat lining was poking him in the side, something which had been there since he had been woken up by the screaming Miss Collett, and had until now remained ignored. His gaze was still on the handkerchief as he put his fingers into his coat, reaching inwards. Embroidered on the inside of the white-red cloth was the initials **P.B.**

He reached down inside the coat lining and closed his hand around something metal.

There was a dagger in his pocket.

***

Sullivan opened the bathroom door, eyes blazing, and strode towards the centre of the carriage, gaze fixed on Miss Collett.

'Everything alright, Marshal?' Mr Nethercott asked anxiously, in the midst of taking a break from smoking his pipe as Sullivan placed himself in the picture.

'Splendid,' said Sullivan as he averted the gaze of everyone but Miss Collett. 'Miss Collett here was busy doing her makeup at the far end of the carriage in the mirror at the same time as the murder.' He watched her countenance for any hint of conciliation or calculation; any sign that she was a manipulator behind this scheme. 'I'm happy to vouch for her innocence.'

Her eyes widened and darted from Marshal to Sergeant, but other than that she kept her countenance. Mr Nethercott seemed unaware that anything was amiss.

'Marvellous,' he declared, as though Sullivan had been a doctor taking Miss Collett's temperature after a dizzy spell and found her quite recovered. 'Then that's all the likely suspects crossed off the list. It's never the most obvious of people.'

Sullivan edged a little further to the woman, who looked on the verge of bolting for the window. 'Actually, I was hoping to have a word with her.' His gaze gave her no option to refuse. 'Just a quick follow up.'

She quickly stood up and accompanied him to the end of the carriage and into the conductor's cabin, where they took the closed cubicle and hid out of sight.

He waited almost a full minute before speaking, trying to get the measure of her.

'I know it's you,' he began before she could say anything. 'The letter, Patrick Blake, all of it…You've been in England for two weeks. I know who's payroll you're on. You've stolen memory-transfer blueprints for the French government.' Her eyebrows shot into the back of her head and her mouth opened wide to cry out. He held up a hand. 'Please, don't try to deny it. We only have so much time.'

He showed her the dagger, along with the embroidered handkerchief still covered in blood. 'This knife,' he said, pointing at it, 'it's police issue.'

She could only stare at him.

'Which means, you're not the murderer. You were sat down talking to the ticket inspector while the victim was locked inside the bathroom.'

She said nothing,

'Did I do it?' he demanded of her. 'Am I Patrick Blake?' He held her in an intense stare to look for any sign that she was lying. Her eyes were large and afraid. Did he know her? Did she know him? All of this seemed so familiar, like an unremembered dream that at the time felt like the most important memory to cling on to. 'Tell me,' he smashed his hand against the door, making it rattle.

'I don't know,' she burst out all at once. He raised his fists as she stammered. 'Please, honestly, I don't. My memory has been wiped, same as yours. I can't even remember what I'm doing in this country.'

Sullivan let out a cry and drew away from her, clenching his fists to lock them in place. He turned to her, eyes squinting into slits.

'But the letter…' he enveloped her in his accusations. 'You are the spy, the one they're talking about in the paper. It's you.' A finger jabbed at her, 'And you were with someone. Correct? An accomplice.'

Those big brown eyes watched him in horror. Her whole body was shaking, her breath creeping through in long, shuddering rattles. She nodded.

'And he was an officer, correct? That's what the report said.'

She nodded again.

'Then there's only one explanation.'

He watched in dismay as her head bobbed up and down a third time.

'You seem familiar,' she said, 'in a way I can't quite put my finger on. Am I the same to you? How do we know? Is all memory of our relationship truly wiped away, even if we had spent a hundred years in each other's company?'

'Consciously, yes,' said Sullivan, 'but it cannot completely strip away all memory. Thought, touch, dreams and sensations, all unconscious memory stays.'

She put her hand back in his pocket and drew closer to him. 'And have you dreamt of me, Marshal Sullivan?' she said, as she fluttered her eyelids in mock sincerity. The scent of perfume filled his nostrils.

'I never remember a single dream I ever have,' he replied honestly. 'But…you seem as though you know me. And perhaps I know you?'

'We can but speculate.' She took her hand away from him, and he felt as though he had done something wrong.

He sighed.

Patrick. Was that his name? It was Irish, after all. He knew that much about himself. But why the disguise? Was he even a Marshal? Or was his badge a fake, too? He had memories of his time as a community officer; were all those recollections fabricated as well? All his accolades? His time with Monica? Andrew?

Sullivan took an intake of breath and clasped his hands to his ears. 'How can we not know? Was this our plan all along? Why did we have to murder someone?'

All of a sudden, Sullivan had that feeling a tall person gets when they stand up too quickly, and he was forced into a seat. He sat down, confused by it all, and took off his hat, rubbing his forehead as he used to when he was young and he had been reading for too long.

Miss Collett took his hands in hers.

'I know only what you know. Both our memories are wiped, meaning one thing only, that you decided it was safer for us not to know what was going on. Maybe McClean found out about us, maybe he knew nothing about it. All I know is we are in this together, and if either one of us is caught, the other will not be far behind.'

Sullivan stared at the mirror without listening to her. 'My entire career, I've followed the rules—my whole life.' He looked deep into her eyes, searching for some familiar spark to ignite his memory. 'Why would I give it all away, for you? I don't even know who you are.'

They sat there for a few moments, not knowing what had happened or what was going to happen. Soon it became clear they would have to go back and face the others.

'I don't know who you are either, Mr Sullivan,' Miss Collett muttered, 'All I know is that we have to find a way off this train, or the only memories we'll know of each other will be from the inside of a prison cell.'

They left one after the other; him looking as wiry and professional as when he had exited, and she with a curt upper-lip and a frozen expression of indifference. From their features, one would guess the weather had been the main point of discussion. They had whispered for another five minutes together, keeping one eye on the clock. Sullivan had decided the best course of action was to meticulously examine the minds of each passenger one by one, and waste time until they arrived in London. He would be the first to alert his fellow officers to the murder and excuse himself to write a report, heading to the station along with Miss Collett, claiming her to be in shock, at which point they would board the quickest train to Calais. The two of them would be in France before his absence was reported.

***

'Does anyone else need to use the bathroom?' muttered Mr Nethercott as the two of them returned to the main carriage.

'There seems to be a body in it, if you hadn't heard,' Mr Woolf remarked, sipping his tea.

'Maybe we should move it,' came the reply. 'Cole should move it. Finders keepers, they say.'

'I'm too weak,' protested Mr Cole. He pointed at Mr Woolf. 'He should move it, he's the strongest.'

'Me?' scoffed the businessman. 'I've more years as Caesar has stab wounds. You, my boy, are a young buck. Hop to it.'

'No one is moving the body,' growled Sullivan, glowering at them and putting the bickering to an end.

The air filled with pipe smoke, and finally the pause was broken, as usual, by Mr Woolf. 'Well,' he chipped in before the silence could settle, 'that's everyone, isn't it? It looks like we're all innocent.' Everyone looked around the room, all thinking the same thing.

Mr Woolf: smoking his pipe.

Jack Jackson: drooling in the corner.

Miss Collett: picking at her cuticles.

Mr Nethercott…

'All except one,' said Miss Collett, looking at the Sergeant.

There was a pause as the proverbial penny dropped.

Mr Woolf chuckled. 'Come now, mademoiselle,' he said light-heartedly, 'Mr Nethercott is an esteemed officer of the law. A fine joke of yours, the sarcasm of which was no doubt lost on its intended subject.'

'Sir, you can take me seriously,' Miss Collett explained. 'We all want the truth to come out, no?'

She shot a glance over Mr Woolf's shoulder to Sullivan, standing behind him. He caught her meaning. A frame would not work in the long term, but casting enough doubt over the authorities about Mr Nethercott's involvement, considering that he was responsible for the captive, would give them enough time to slip away.

'If you don't mind me saying so, Mr Nethercott,' said Sullivan, wafting away the smoke billowing from the two gentlemen's pipes, 'you don't seem overly concerned that your captive has been murdered.'

The laughter suddenly died as Mr Nethercott began to bristle like an overused comb. 'Well, I never,' he began, 'ever would assume to speak to another official in such a manner. Whatever has gotten into you, my dear fellow?'

Sullivan asked the question again, unimpressed at his attempt to save face in front of his new business companion. It was at this moment that Miss Collett decided to take his side.

'What reason could you have to refuse unless you were guilty?' She let the accusation hang in the air. A glance passed between her and Sullivan, unnoticed by the others.

'Excuse me, miss,' Mr Nethercott's eyebrows became so knotted they were in danger of joining forces, 'but in this country, we—'

'May I remind you, sir,' interrupted Sullivan, 'that a refusal to submit to a memory inspection is an arrestable offence. Your status as officer does not exempt you.'

'Nothing to hide, nothing to fear, eh Marshal?' sneered Mr Nethercott, refusing to take the bait. 'I never thought I'd see the day when such crude pseudo-authority was cast over fellow officers wearing Her Majesty's uniform.' He extended his hand, beckoning for Sullivan to approach him. 'Here, then, inspect my mind, if it'll put your paranoid one at ease.'

Sullivan took a step, reaching down to hand over an uploader, when Mr Nethercott darted forwards and snatched something out of his pocket. He danced away, waving the blood-coated handkerchief in the air like a captured flag. 'Ah ha!'

Sullivan froze.

Mr Woolf and Mr Cole jumped to their feet, both crying out at the imminent violence on display.

'I thought I saw a flash of red earlier,' hissed Mr Nethercott, his eyes narrowed into slits. 'Glad to see my vision still hasn't failed me.'

'What's going on here?' demanded Mr Woolf, raising from his seat with the speed of a man ready to use his fists.

'It would appear that Marshal Sullivan,' began Mr Nethercott, 'has wiped his own memory.'

Mr Woolf's eyes were set to burst out of his skull. 'What?'

'It's quite the defence, isn't it?' he continued, waving his arms around the vicinity, as though by doing so he could summon all logic to his side. 'How can you confess to something you don't remember?'

Sullivan shook his head. 'You must be out of your mind.'

'But you said it yourself, Marshal,' Mr Nethercott reminded him. 'It had to have been someone in this room. The bathroom was locked from the inside, and we five are the only ones here. We've checked the memory of everyone else. Everyone but you.'

Miss Collett moved to sit behind Sullivan, afraid of an outburst from either party.

Mr Cole went to hide behind Mr Nethercott and Mr Woolf.

'You want to know my theory?' continued Mr Nethercott, 'I think you're not a Marshal at all, but a French informant.'

Miss Collett let out an exclamation that sounded terribly French. 'An informant? Does he sound like a Frenchman to you, sir?'

'Protect him all you like,' he jeered, 'I saw the way you two walked off together. Do you really expect us to believe this is the first time you've met? Look at them, it's obvious,' he waved a hand in their direction to dismiss any notion of their innocence. 'They knew McClean would be on board this train. They planned to kill him before he could confess his collusion with the French. Here, right in front of us, is the evidence of the phony peace our "allies" have forced on us. What kind of peace is it when your enemies murder and rob from their betters? Why, I bet if we checked the Marshal's memory cleaner right now, it would still be warm from the exercise of removing all knowledge of his own betrayal.'

Sullivan glanced from pair-to-pair of suspicious eyes and saw the expressions accompanying them shift from furrowed looks of confusion into comprehending frowns. He could only remain silent, powerless to stop the others from drawing the conclusion they would inevitably reach.

'That's quite the story,' Sullivan fingered his moustache momentarily, knowing that his next few words must be chosen with care, 'coming from a man trying to cover-up his own disgrace.'

Mr Nethercott's hair almost stood on end at his words. They could see the Thames veering up out of the window, and the factories had been passing by for some time now. It would not be long before they arrived.

'If it was I who let an Old Bailey captive die on my watch,' said Sullivan, tip-toeing around the evidence against him, 'I'd be worried about showing my face to my superiors. So worried, in fact, that I might even go so far as to frame a fellow officer as complicit in my own blunder.'

Mr Nethercott's face scrunched-up in fury. 'You don't want to continue talking to me in that manner.' His hand began to slide towards his belt as he spoke. 'If I were you, I wouldn't make accusations I wasn't prepared to back-up.'

Sullivan's hand similarly slid down to the bottom of his waistcoat. 'The same could be said about making threats.' His fingers danced over the holster, itching to get at the pistol waiting patiently inside.

All eyes were fixed on the two of them. The two officers, about to face-off in a Manchester to London carriageway. Where was a ticket inspector when you needed one?

Mr Woolf threw up his arms and stepped forward between the two men. 'Why don't we all calm down for a second, yes?' He looked at both men with a face which begged for nothing but good intentions. 'We're about to arrive from what's been a very stressful journey. I am sure we can look over this drama as a result of high tensions and chafed egos after we have sorted everything out with the authorities. What do you say?' He looked imploringly at the pair.

Right then, the automatic announcer boomed over the speakers:

'Now arriving at, London, King's Cross. We hope you have enjoyed your journey.'

'I've heard enough,' scoffed Sullivan, pushing Mr Woolf out of the way. 'Sergeant Nethercott, you're under arrest—'

Blood spattered against Mr Woolf's tweed suit as the bang echoed through the carriageway.

The bullet shaved-off the top of Sullivan's right ear, knocking his hat askew and sending him reeling while his head rang with the sound of the gunshot.

'No!' bellowed Mr Woolf, throwing himself at the officer before he could fire a second shot and knocking his gun flying in the air. It landed by Miss Collett's feet.

At that moment, the doors burst open, and they saw a panicking crowd, some of whom had heard the gunshot, while others hurried on to the ticket barrier unaware. Sullivan saw his chance and turned, fleeing towards the exit. He glanced back to see Mr Nethercott and Mr Woolf tangling on the ground, then looked up just in time to crash into something in front of him. It was Jack Jackson, who had finally left his seat and tried to get away from the loud noise in blind fear, walking into everything in front of him like a woodlouse.

'Imbecile,' cried Sullivan, untangling himself and throwing the limp body to the ground. His eyes rolled like those of a fallen horse, and suddenly he seemed strangely familiar. Sullivan had no time to dwell on the recognition, however, as Mr Nethercott would soon be upon him.

He dashed towards the exit, nothing to stop him from leaving now.

Sullivan hammered on the open button, before jumping out and running head first into Miss Collett.

The two of them nearly toppled over, but she managed to grab him and steady both of them.

'What are you—'

She shot him in the stomach.

'Uuf.'

Sullivan frowned, looking down at the hollow wound in his midriff, groaned, and slumped down to the floor.

The crowd was screaming now and running in all directions.

Miss Collett stood over him, saying nothing. Mr Nethercott's gun was still smoking in her hand. She dropped it to the ground as soon as shouts and flashing lights started to appear outside the station windows.

And then, all of a sudden, perhaps because of the extreme trauma his mind was experiencing, perhaps because of some technological error, Sullivan remembered everything. He reached down, taking hold of the bloody handkerchief, and passed it over to Miss Collett. She took it numbly.

'Mademoiselle,' he said, and died.

Miss Collett put a hand into Sullivan's pocket as he lay dead, reached inside and brought out the uploader containing her recollections of the letter. She crushed it under her heel just as the police sirens began to drown out the sound of the screaming crowd. She slumped next to Sullivan's body, laying on the ground, and waited for the police to arrive.

***

The police arrived in Carriage A to find a dead Marshal, a murdered Scotsman, an injured Sergeant and a Frenchwoman with an officer's pistol by her side. Needless to say, there were a lot of questions that needed answering

All of the party were immediately arrested, including Mr Nethercott, in spite of his protests. Miss Collett was held the longest, until they could determine that she had been acting in self-defence. Sergeant Nethercott vouched for her intervention and cleared her of all charges. She was promised safe passage back to France as long as she signed a letter promising to never publicly speak of her involvement in the nation-wide scandal. Officials could not stop the details of the case from spilling over to the media at large, however

The murder weapon was quickly found in the Marshal's pocket, and the police quickly agreed that he had been the French agent responsible for the murder.

Miss Collett was given a free pass, and told that no charges would be levied against her, on the condition that she signed an agreement not to talk to the press.

Newspapers filled train stations and shop fronts with photos of the murdered inventor, stuck next to pictures of the turncoat Marshal, who had gone by the alias Sullivan. Interviews with Sergeant Nethercott, promoted days after the incident, accompanied the scandal of a man betraying his nation, turning against Queen and country, all for the promise of French money in exchange for handing over a full-memory transfer prototype. No stories about Callum McClean could be found amongst the headlines. Already yesterday's news, the murder of Britain's most famous inventor was quickly forgotten.

Mr Nethercott gained a knighthood for his discovery of the plan hatched by a fellow law enforcer to betray his comrades and sell memory tech to an enemy nation. Inquiries were made about the loyalty of the newly conquered state and the shaky alliance which existed between the two nations. Although officially the memory prototype was announced as secured by British officers, the plans were never found, and no documents at the Marshal's home confirmed their whereabouts.

Mr Cole received an award for his bravery in deciding to keep the train on route to safety despite the hijacking. Michael Cole would continue to operate trains long into his old age, when he would become a household name for the Railway Industry Association. He would become something of an embarrassment in later years, where he was often talked over at events and condescended to by younger conductors, who had heard the story of Carriage A dozens of times before.

Mr Woolf apologised over and over again in the police station for his mistaken defence of the disgraced Marshal, begging officers not to charge him with abetting the man. Given a stern warning, Mr Woolf was shooed away from the scene and told how lucky he was that Sergeant Nethercott did not want to press charges. As an apology, Mr Nethercott would receive stock in Woolf & Co for another three years, until the overvaluation of railroads caused steel value to plummet and Woolf & Co collapsed into insolvency alongside the East India Company. Sabastian Woolf would spend years depressed and alone, considering himself a failure, until a half-decade later when his contacts in Paris and investments in French memory transfer technology would make him a rich man until the end of his days.

Lastly, Jack Jackson, the vagrant from Manchester, who could neither be called a participant in the events nor witness to them, was released as soon as his head was found to contain no memory whatsoever, and was thrown out on to the streets. Wandering aimlessly for days, he was set upon by fellow beggars. They kicked his lifeless body and laughed at his weak attempts to fend off their blows. Bored, they soon ransacked his pockets to look for silver coins or leftover food. Delighted, they soon found the engagement ring stuffed in the man's front pocket and hooted with glee as they tossed away the box and took the right.

A shining memory-uploader fell out of Jack Jackson's front pocket and on to the floor, with the name 'Sullivan' written on the side. Confused, the beggar, sweeping his greasy locks aside, sniffed the uploader for tampering and then screwed the metal rod into the back of his head, hoping that it was some hastily recorded sex-memory or that it might reveal a hidden stash of opium nearby.

Instead, memories of sitting aboard the Manchester to London express, Carriage A, flooded through the beggar's head.

***

...As you will no doubt be aware, the inventor has been murdered and his plans stolen. They have been destroyed, but committed to memory; a memory we will uncover in Paris together. If everything has gone according to plan, you will have been questioned by the police and released, while the suspect will be behind bars awaiting execution. But the real murderer, I, who have written this confession, will soon be by

your side. You have no memory of this, or of me, because I have wiped both of our memories to protect you. You will know how to find me after you are out of danger, and find me you must, for as long as we are separated, I shall forever be miserable.

Your friend and lover,
Patrick Blake

Patrick folded the letter carefully, scribbling on the front to make sure Elisabeth would not open it until they were both safe in London, and hid it at the bottom of her bag. He had wiped her memory a few minutes ago, after he had found and murdered McClean.

He could see the train conductor trying to unscrew the lock at the front of the carriage. He would find the body in a few moments. Patrick had slid the lock back in place from the outside using a key, making it look as though it was locked from the inside. As soon as he was sure nobody was watching, Patrick stood up and walked over to the front of the train carriage where the greying Marshal was sat staring out of the window.

He knew he only had a few moments.

'Excuse me, Mr Sullivan' Patrick sat down next to the man in uniform, ignoring his look of annoyance at being interrupted from his thoughts.

'Can I help you?' the Marshal raised an eyebrow at Patrick and shuffled away in a disgruntled wriggle.

'I hope so. I would never normally offer this, but I was wondering if you needed a handkerchief? You seem to have such a terrible cold.'

The Marshal nodded, covering his nose with his hand.

'Thank you ever so kindly.'

Patrick reached into his pocket to produce the garment, but as he handed it to him, he saw the white linens were stained bright red. 'Sorry,' he exclaimed, 'I've just murdered a man, you see, and I do hate to leave a mess.'

The Marshal's trained hand darted towards his gun, but it was caught fast by Patrick's snaring grasp. Marshal Sullivan looked up just in time to see a memory cleaner aimed directly between his eyes, taken from his own holster.

'Wait—'

Zap.

The deed was done. The Marshal fell back against his chair with his eyes closed and his tongue lolling out. Patrick wiped the bloody knife he had used to kill McClean on the handkerchief and placed both of them in the Marshal's pockets. He looked around to see if anyone had noticed him, but there was no one to be seen. Patrick eased the Marshal into a comfortable position. It would be roughly 15 minutes before he woke up again with no memory of what had happened.

Patrick walked away as quickly as he had arrived and sat back down next to Elisabeth, the love of his life, and the woman he was going to ask to marry him. Knowing what was coming, he placed his fake identification number in his front pocket, and found a comfortable position.

Jack Jackson, read the fake citizen ID.

Patrick planted a kiss on her forehead, then sat in the aisle opposite so they would not attract suspicion as companions. *Farewell my love*, he pressed the memory suppressor to his temple, angling it outside the window so it would fall from his grip and be lost to the countryside as soon as his memory was gone. Patrick set the level to the maximum and imagined waking up to that beautiful face with a view of Paris behind her. *May you never forget me.*

He hit the trigger.

Revolutions of the Heavenly Spheres

'Name?'

The dark figure swivelled the lamp so it was pointed in Eric's face, the large white orb circling around him.

'Eric Cuspon.'

The figure lit a cigarette, lanky hair and a broken nose becoming visible for a few moments before a fat thumb extinguished the flame.

'Real name?'

'I think you know the answer to that, else I wouldn't be here.'

An intake of breath followed the pause.

'Do you know why you're here?'

The man opposite him drew on the cigarette while Eric waited, smoke wafting up to engulf the broken ceiling fan.

'That sounds like a law enforcement question. Though, I must say, it's refreshing to hear it while handcuffed to a studio chair instead of a police table.'

Click.

The man cocked a pistol, placed it on the table in front, and waited a few minutes while he finished his cigarette.

'Okay, Eric,' he went on, 'Here's how this is going to work. I'm going to ask you a few questions about the night of January 29, 1987. Then you're going to answer them for me. You're being recorded, and believe me when I say I'll know if you're lying.'

'I don't deny my involvement.'

'Good—then this will be quicker than I thought. Water?'

'No, thank you.'

'Right. Make sure you're ready. And don't mumble.'

Eric nodded.

'From the beginning. Tell me about January 29.'

He took a breath.

'Alright, picture it. You're living in a cheap flat in the east end. You haven't had work for the better part of two months. Out of the blue, you hear about a very specific job. 160 memories, one take. All reconstructions, owned by a private collector named Alessandro Rinier. They're mostly blurry reconstructions, pieced together from decayed brain matter. Some of them are originals—few of the earliest memory storage devices ever created. And there's a couple of real juicy numbers. A 14-year reconstruction of Dante's last years, ages 42 to 55. A few early memories of Galileo's, a smattering of Newton and Da Vinci, and the crown jewels: a 1566 original of Copernicus' complete thoughts and memories, first edition, worth about a quarter of a million on its own. You might even get two million for it on the clean market.'

He continued, 'Now, I know what you're thinking. Too good to be true, right? But here's the best bit. January 29th, for one night only, all 160 upload uploaders are to be held in a warehouse in Feltham ahead of the 1st California International Antiquarian Memory Fair where they're due to be flown to the next day. This is coming from a guy on the inside, is what I'm told. It's a three-person job: one guy in the warehouse, one in the van and one on the roof. The two other guys are solid enough. Nate was an Upstate New Yorker. Completely illiterate, but one hell of a safe-cracker; you don't get too many like him anymore. It's all memory-hacking nowadays.'

He added, 'Our van guy was this Italian fellow called Lalo. I'd worked with Lalo before on an embassy job. He'd been in the police force, even had a few connections there. He was also a deaf-mute. Some people say that made him harder to work with, I'd say it made it easier. The more you talk on a job, the less focused you are on getting it done, 'least in my experience.'

'And your employer?'

'Never met the guy.'

'Not once? Hard to believe.'

'It's a policy that Aaron had. He was the handler. Knew him from business school—Aaron made sure he was the only one who contacted our employer, for all the good it did him. They called him "The Astronomer", that's all I ever heard about him.'

'The Astronomer? Peculiar nickname, isn't it?'

'Funny you should say so, you lot ought to be familiar with him. Detectives started calling him that on account of all the old-world astrology memories he was interested in. He was fascinated by the universe, Aaron would say, wanted to visit every planet there was, taste every star. I even heard he was a body snatcher, 200 years old, if you believe in that rubbish.'

'But you never met him? Never heard him speak?'

'Nobody has, so far as I know.'

'Huh.'

'So, we lift the books and make off within two hours, easy as you like. We're on our way back to Aaron's office with £2.5 million in the back and three fat grins on our faces. Not much more to tell at this point, you'd think? Well, you'd be wrong. We see smoke coming from Aron's office, check the news and see there's been a gas leak. That's when the second explosion hit. You could have heard it at the top of the shard. By the time we arrive, the place is crawling end-to-end with fire engines and coppers. Quite the coincidence, don't you think?'

'What did you do?'

'What could we do? We knew that by tomorrow a list of the stolen books would be on every front page in the world. Reputable dealers and collectors wouldn't touch them, so we split them three ways:

'Nate got Date's best years, specifically the 12 years he spent writing the *Divine Comedy*, along with a good chunk of other bits and bobs. Lalo insisted on taking the original Galileo; he made a point of it—maybe he knew something we didn't, you know?'

The lamplight twinkled off the glistening gun as the shrouded man swayed it from side to side, nodding. The light from its oily barrel began to vanish as he retracted it, as though tempted to hide behind the safety of the lamp.

'And me? I took the Copernicus. Nate thought he was getting the better deal, went for the most valuable one. But the real price of anything is what somebody's willing to pay for it. Then, we ran. None of us stayed together. The less of us there were, the less chance we had of all getting caught. That was the last time I saw either of them.'

'Forgive me for interrupting, but your companions…Did you ever discover what happened to Lalo and Nate? I've a tough time believing you never tried to contact them.'

'Oh, I tried, but the Peelers caught up with Lalo. He never even got out of London. He's doing a lifetime stint in Pentonville right now, God help him. After that, it was too risky. Shame, good driver. Nate probably had the most luck out of any of us. He managed to find a dealer within a few days for the Dante piece, so I heard.'

'And how did you get away?'

'Well, I'm getting to that. It's five in the morning, January 30th, with 70 years of Copernicus rattling around the inside of my bag. My guess is whoever hired us was after the years Copernicus spent writing *De Revolutionibus Orbium Coelestium*, worth £215,000, remember? So, I'm thinking I can get that to him some other way, cut it off from the main piece, then find a buyer on my own for the rest. My plan is to head to Warsaw, lie low for a bit, then hit up a few old black-memory contacts. I'm on my way to the station to get out of the city, when I hear this panting sound coming from a nearby alley, like someone whimpering. I've always been too curious for my own good.'

He continued, 'I turn the corner and see a dog lying in the alley with both of its back legs broken—looked as though it'd been there for a while. The mewing gets louder the closer I get and he tries to shuffle away. I grab hold of his collar, and there's a note attached to it which says:

"HI. MY NAME IS ROGER. PLEASE RING THIS NUMBER IF I GET LOST: 07841 395566."

'I've always had a thing for dogs. If it had been a cat, I would have walked on by; wouldn't have given it a second thought. But you can't just leave a poor mutt to bleed on the street, can you? So, I got out my phone. I remember the number on the collar, too. It ended in double-five double-six. For a second nobody answers. I'm about to walk on by, when a sharp white noise bursts out of my phone and it stings me— like gripping an electric fence—and it drops on the floor. As soon as I bend to pick it up, I feel something cold pressing against my head, followed by a click and someone behind me saying "don't turn around".'

He added, 'Before I do anything, he lowers the gun to the ground. I feel the weight leave my neck, and then he points it towards Roger and shoots the mutt in the belly. My face is wet from the spray. He tells me to get on my knees, using my real name. That was what really scared me about the guy; he knew something nobody is supposed to know. "It's a beautiful night," he says to me. "I need you to look up and start counting. Count the stars up there for me, please, and tell me how far you get." I look up, glad that I don't have to watch whatever's left of Roger. Then I hear him cock the pistol all the way down, and I do as I'm told:

'One…Two…

'I feel something wet trickling against my leg.

'12…13…

'I want to look down, but if I do I know he'll kill me.

'116…

'By the end of it, I felt this numb, peaceful feeling wash over me, like a wave you didn't see coming.

'1317…

66

'I made sure I didn't miss a single star. When I'm done, I turn around, expecting to feel a bullet in my innards, and he's disappeared along with the stolen memory of Copernicus. I never saw his face.'

'Who was he? The man who stole from you?'

'You know who he was.'

'You think he was the Astronomer?'

'Yes.'

'How can you know?'

'I just know. It was the way he moved, the way he talked, it was all calculated. Anything I could have said or done, he'd already thought of it. That night had been planned before any of us even got the call for the job.'

'So, what happened next?'

'Nothing.'

'What do you mean nothing?'

'I got the next flight to Warsaw and hid here ever since, looking for the occasional post-office job.'

'You mean, that's it?'

'What were you expecting? The strangest thing was that after all that, I find a buyer here in Warsaw who'd been asking around after the lift. I'd be rolling in cash right about now if the job had gone down like it was supposed to, but that was exactly how he planned it, I imagine. Thieves have fewer avenues of recourse than the law abiding. It was 9096, by the way.'

'I beg your pardon?'

'That's the number of stars I counted. Funny, isn't it? You'd think that—'

The giant, luminous lamp was thrown against the wall and shattered, leaving the lonely cigarette floating in darkness.

Then a switch turned on, and light streamed into the room, drowning both of them under luminous rays.

'I guess there's no point hiding any longer.'

Eric blinked the light out of his eyes.

'Lalo?'

There he was. Clearer than crystal.

'Uh-huh, good to see you, Eric. Pity it's not under better circumstances.'

'I thought you were locked up...or dead—you can *talk*?'

'Evidently so. I thought you of all people would have guessed the deaf-mute thing was just an act. Never told people I was, anyway. I just never talked on jobs as a rule. Funny, the assumptions people make. I'm still no closer to finding out what really happened that night. Sorry about the kidnapping; it had to be done, you see. I couldn't be certain you weren't involved. Hang on, I'll uncuff you.'

The handcuffs clattered to the floor, Eric rubbed his wrists and let out a grateful sigh.

'Don't take it personally, but you couldn't have been easier to pick up. Paper trail was so obvious that at first, I thought you wanted me to find you. Surprised to see me, huh? I'll bet; the bastard nearly got me too.'

'The Astronomer? Our employer?'

'Whoever he was. On the way out of London, I'm stopped in the middle of the street by a Spanish lady telling me she's just been roughed up by some creeps. She asks if I can ring her husband for her—I've always hated it when guys rough up girls. My phone stings me as soon as I type in the number, same as you, and it drops to the pavement. When I look up, I see her laying on the ground.

'That's when I feel that cold metal against the back of my skull and hear that prick's voice in my ear, "Look up," he says. "I need you to start counting. Tell me how high you get." He takes every manuscript I had straight out of my satchel and leaves me bone dry. The only reason I got away was because a cop-car pulled up outside the alley, and he scarpers. They take me in cuffs, but they don't find my DNA at the scene.' Lalo waved fingered gloves in front of his face. 'I say I found it by the bin. They can't prove I took anything, but I have a flick knife in my pocket, so I do six months in the can. Maximum sentence. Pentonville is the worst jail I've been in, I'll tell you that for free, but it stopped me from getting a bullet in the head.'

'The number? Did it end in double-five double-six?'

'Yeah, it did—the same number as was on the dog's collar.'

'How high did you get?'

'Huh?'

'With the stars, how high did you get?'

'What do you care? I was busy stopping my skull from getting opened up.'

'Nate must have been in on it, Lalo. He's the only one who could have known our routes. It's the only thing that makes—'

'Nate's dead, Eric.'

That gave him pause.

'What now?'

'He never made it out of London. Philip, the guy who tipped us off about the job? Dead too, along with Aaron and everyone who worked for him. There's just us left.'

'But I thought…'

69

'Me too. I heard the same you did, except I found him before the peelers got me. He'd been in a Whitehall dumpster for about 12 hours. He had two bullet holes in him, and a scar sliced into his back with a knife.'

'A scar?'

'Yeah, writing, like someone had cut a message for me to find.'

'What did he write?'

'It was a number: 9093…No clue what it meant.'

'He must have missed three.'

'What?'

'Three stars—three bullet holes. He must have made him count.'

Lalo paced around the room, hand to his beard.

'Whoever he was, he wasn't working for the Astronomer. He had a letter with him from Alessandro Rinier, the book dealer. It wasn't the Astronomer we were working for, Eric, it was Rinier—we just didn't know it. Nate got greedy and thought he could make more money selling the Dante memories to Rinier's partners. That's how they knew about the job, and why they planted C4 under Aaron's office.'

Eric took out a handkerchief and dabbed at his eyes, the white embroidering dancing in the light. 'But—so Nate thought he could undercut the Astronomer by selling the manuscripts back to the shareholders?'

'The Astronomer isn't real, Eric, he's just a spook name. The guy who came after us just wanted Rinier's money back. "The Astronomer" is what detectives liked to call him, but he's just a gang of hitmen hired by art dealers, and hitmen like to have a reputation. Rinier found out about the job once Nate started talking and sent someone after us. We were stealing the book for Aaron, not for any "Astronomer". Why do you think we never met the guy?'

'That explains a lot, but not everything…Why leave me or you alive? Everybody else who took the job is dead.'

Lalo shrugged.

'I can't be sure—maybe they only wanted to get Nate for trying to play both sides? Maybe not. Prick must have thought neither of us was worth the risk; guess we'll never really be sure.'

'All this time…Aaron must have put millions into that job. Rinier, too. It's a shame we've got nothing to show for it, quite the anti-climax.'

'Well, it's funny you should say that…'

Lalo unzipped his rucksack and unsheathed a memory uploader. It was dated 1566 with a museum tag dangling from its tip.

'You're kidding me.'

'Nope. Eight of Galileo's finest years, the exact ones he spent writing *Dialogue Concerning the Two Chief World Systems,* in fact, though with a slight watermark. I pushed it down the drain before the cops could get to me. Soon as I'm out, I head straight down into the sewers, and what do you know? It's caught in the filter leading out into the Thames— sanitation workers will never know how much money they'd have made if they'd been doing their jobs properly. Before tracking you down, I looked for a buyer on my own. I'd heard rumours of something going on in Latin America. There are huge colonies over there, running from Brazil to Mexico, set up by body snatchers. Someone told me through the grapevine about people from that world looking for black-market memory on astronomy, but as soon as I start asking questions the trail goes cold. But, looks like I was looking in the wrong part of the world. I've got a product; you've got a buyer. I don't see any reason you and I can't do business one last time.'

'You know what Lalo? It's as if you read my mind.'

The door creaked open, and light streamed into the room, chasing the dark away, so one could not tell where the sun started and the reflections began.

They headed towards the door, giggling like school girls. Eric stretched and rubbed his hands with glee, while the younger man beamed and beckoned for him to pass over the buyer's number.

'What's your guy's number again?' He read off the scrap of paper. 'Three, nine, five…five, six, six.'

It wasn't quite morning when they got outside and walked under clear skies. The roads were empty and the streets were filled with discarded cans and cigarette packets. The stars were shining bright, brighter than anything you could look at underneath them.

'Lalo, there's one thing still bothering me, about all of this…about the Astronomer and everything,' said Eric, watching him. 'Something you never answered.'

'Yeah? What might that be? Ah!'

The phone let out an electric charge and clattered to the ground, with Lalo hissing in pain.

'Bastard, it stung me! Throw-away phones, eh? Piece of junk.'

Lalo bent over to reach for it.

'What was it you were gonna ask?'

Click.

'Lalo, how high did you get?'

A Dog Called Ego

The shouting grew louder.

Cathy paused and swept the hair out of her face. The sound of shrieking picked up around the corner from her flat. One of the junk-memory users from Block A was shouting at his girlfriend to go home and see her children. His girlfriend was crying and shouting so loudly that Cathy couldn't make out a single word.

She put her hood up and pushed her hair back again when she saw a man with his hands in his pockets about to walk past her. Cathy had changed out of the pencil skirt and high-heeled boots she wore to work, swapping them for baggy jeans and a hoodie, wriggling into them on the train home.

Before heading to work this morning, Cathy had walked past a man who always wore a grey jumper with the hood tied so tightly around his chin that you could only see his eyes. She suspected this was an attempt to cover the burn marks that scarred the left-hand side of his face, sealing his right eye shut in its socket. Tonight, the man walking towards her was wearing a similar hoody, but it was too dark to see who it might be.

The shouting grew more audible.

'...not fit to be in my house...'

He was whistling loudly, but it was hard to hear him over the yelling coming from the building opposite. This made her think it was someone other than the burnt man, who did not seem the type to draw attention to himself.

"...rather take junk uploads than take care of your own kids, you're a mess..."

The woman's cry slowly became more decipherable, morphing into a long, drawn-out stutter, stretching the word "fuck" halfway between a moan and a scream.

F-F-F-FFUUUUCCCKKKK-K.

She walked past the man with her hood up, eyes down, wondering if she would catch a glimpse of burned, dead skin for the second time today.

A familiar face greeted her as he passed under the light that lit the corridor. He smiled at her, his eyebrows shooting up. She dropped her eyes, pretending not to have looked up at him and walked on. He had told her his name the first time they were in the lift together on the way up to the flat, but she was bad with names. He had asked her what her job was. She told him that she was a reporter; "*journalist*" always seemed too senior, too show-offy. But he'd seemed impressed, anyway. She had mumbled a thank you and asked him what he did for a living. He'd told her he got up every morning at 3:00 am to go down to the skip to look for metal, which he sold to people that lived in the woods. She had made a joke about collecting toy soldiers when she had been a kid. He'd laughed and said he still collected toy soldiers; he still had a collection of toy models he had been collecting for years, and anyway, would she like to come back to his room and have a look at them?

That was when the lift door had opened. She'd told him that sounded nice, but she was very busy and had work to do. He'd looked at the floor and scrunched his face up before hurrying away.

Cathy did not take the lift anymore.

Over the past eight months she'd been living in Block B. The other occupants of the square had invited Cathy to dinner, their room, or a quickie round the corner. Her list of admirers included a homeless woman, another memory junky with half his teeth missing, a single dad, a man in a wheelchair and a 14-year-old named Tyler.

Cathy buzzed herself in with the fob and checked the electricity meter to see if there would be enough for her to shower in the morning. She pulled her jumper tighter around her and walked up the steps, letting herself in.

F-F-FFUUUCCKKK faded away as she slammed the door. Cathy fell into a chair without bothering to turn on the lights. She was too tired to move but knew she should eat. She had skipped both breakfast and lunch today, again, eating only the few snacks brought in by the other reporters.

It was the last day of her probation period tomorrow, and then *The Column* would have to decide if they had enough of a budget for a deputy editor or not. They had already fired two other reporters, and Cathy was brand new to the role, surviving off a recommendation. She had already borrowed more money off her friends than she knew how to pay back, and couldn't afford to pay next month's rent unless they decided to keep her on. One of her source interviews had been cancelled, and another two of her stories had been covered by rival newspapers, meaning that she had missed her daily quota again.

That was when Nez had called her.

She looked at the memory uploader in her hand, biting her lip at the memory of it, or rather, inside it. One of the junk-memory users round the block had given it to her. She had saved the money from the skipped meals to pay her off. She had thought it might not be much more than a sob story piece, but the woman had been in the army—it could have done well with their readers.

'You're gonna want this one for the front pages,' the woman had said, eyes rolling. 'I'm getting no help from the government; no help at all.'

But it hadn't panned out, only giving her quick images of self-harm. Something only a sadist would be interested in reading about. Now, her only other lead was Nez, and she only wanted to call him if she had no other choice.

He picked up the phone immediately.

'18 are still alive,' Nez's voice crackled over the memory phone. 'Almost half.' She heard barking coming from the background and winced. 'You need to be here by five. I'm calling the police then.'

'I'll be there,' she said, staring at the floor as she walked on. 'I told you, I'll be on time. Hold them off as long as you can.'

She needed something for the front page of *The Column*. They didn't have anything for the morning, and she needed something big.

'See you at five,' said Nez, who hung up.

She shook herself. It was time to make a late-night cup of tea. Cathy walked into the kitchen and put the kettle on. Her fridge was full of rotting groceries she had not found time to cook. The freezer door still hadn't been fixed and the window had been left open all day in the middle of winter. She checked her bag to see how many cigarettes she had left and was appalled to find that only two remained.

Her phone lit up with a message from Nez. It said simply:

21 Spindles Farm, Hyde Heath, Buckinghamshire. 12 dead dogs.

Cathy stared at the message. Another one had died. Nez was part of a detox unit, a private clean-up company who were hired to clean up messy incidents after the police were done with them. Usually that meant a meth lab, a suicide or homicide, but a lot of the time, as Cathy had found out, they were called to clean up after cases of animal neglect. They had met nearly a year ago when she had covered an inquest into the death of Atzi Maseualli... Nez's sister. The court found that she had died in childbirth, with no legal responsibility for the state to acknowledge her, as she had entered the country illegally. The child would not obtain British citizenship and would become the responsibility of her closest living relative: Nez.

Nez had looked gaunt and his eyes had been shrunken. He had taken her aside and asked her to leave out any reference to the childbirth. He planned to send the child back to Tenochtitlan, he said, and wanted no attention drawn to them. She had ground her teeth at that. Legally, she'd had every right to publish the details of the woman's death, and every instinct she possessed had urged her to do it. But then she saw his cracked lips, and the red vessels bulging behind his eyes from days of crying; she promised she would leave it out. And so she did.

After she found out he worked with the police, she had given him her number, taken his, and asked him to let her know the night there was something interesting going on. Tonight was that night.

Cathy's room was littered with empty cigarette packages and takeaway boxes. Her old articles were taped to the wall, surrounded by posters of bands she used to like, along with a hole in the middle which used to be filled with couple photos.

On the side of two bookshelves were posters of her favourite journalists next to their breakthrough pieces. William Beauregard, her favourite, was photographed alongside his piece on the Sullivan Memory Scandal. There was Martha Gellhorn, who covered the separatist wars; Nellie Bly, who faked symptoms to pass admission into a lunatic asylum, and, of course, Hunter S. Thompson. Christiane Angelou—her by-line in bold above her scoop on the Astronomer—framed the entire collage underneath.

'You can see this through,' Cathy told herself, looking at the picture of Will Beauregard and Christiane Angelou before switching off the lights—just you wait. She hoped her editor would understand. Cathy threw her camera and notepads into a bag and then took her housemate's keys off the hook. She would return the car in the morning. Just as she left, the shrieking started up again.

***

The raindrops spattered onto the windscreen before they were dashed away by the wipers. The city had faded away, replaced by dotting trees and motorway bridges until London's Shanghai-skyline was a silhouette in her wing mirror. Cathy stuck her little fingers into her eyeball corners and flicked out the sleep crust which had gathered there overnight. She had borrowed her housemate's car without asking again, something she would pay for in the morning. The road kept straying away from her vision, with her eyes slumping towards the windscreen wipers on instinct instead. Cathy was in that foggy, bone-aching state between stirring from bed and being fully awake. It felt as though someone in the night had cut open her head, inserted a rubber band around her brain, then poured sprinkles of sand behind her eyes to make them twinge whenever she looked around. The car heater had not quite kicked in and her breath was fogging up the windscreen. Her decrepit body hunched over the wheel; cold, tired and badly in need of some coffee. She texted while waiting in traffic, letting Nez know she would be there soon.

Her phone blazed into life with a new message, and her breath caught the moment she saw it. She drove on as headlights blurred all around her, fingers twitching toward her phone and distracting her from the road.

What did he say? What did he say? Was he cancelling on her?

She waited till she was waiting to go on to a roundabout and checked the message.

Just me here, was the message that greeted her. *Will have to call police soon. Hurry.*

***

The map showed her dead centred on Piggy Lane, right outside the farmhouse. Dirt roads were replaced with empty fields and rattling wooden gates. She found herself in an open meadow with the silhouette of a looming barn up on the furthest hill, surrounded by a moat of soggy muck. She would have to walk the rest of the way. Cathy turned off the engine, scrambling with her bag to find her phone, and reached for a notepad and pen. As soon as the engine was out cold, she began to hear squelches echoing from the other side of the fence. It was the sound of boots sucking at the mud, the wet dirt clinging to the shuffling rubber soles.

Squelch, squelch.

There was something walking towards her down from the hill. It was a grey, cold morning, with enough mist to blur even the clearest vision.

Squelch, squelch, squelch.

Cathy took a step back from the tree, the birds rustling their feathers up above as she jerked backward, and called out to the being.

'Nez?' she called out.

Squelch, the boots stopped moving.

No reply.

The morning birds began to sing, calling to their younglings to leave the nest and venture away to find what they could to survive the winter. She spotted a pair of hedgehogs playing by an unkempt hedgerow, which out of the corners of her eyes looked like an assortment of writhing worms. A tiny-eyed, hairy face emerged from the ground; a mole emerging from one of its many burrows, pointing its wiggling nose in every direction and scurrying up to greet the orange moon.

The figure began moving again without saying a word, hurrying towards her. It was wearing overalls that hung in loose, baggy patches, making its shape change with every lurch. With an eager pace, the figure sped up as soon as it saw Cathy leaning by the tree.

Squelch, squelch, squelch, squelch.

Cathy backed away. 'Nez!'

The shuffling mass swung the gate open with bullish force, swerving its body around and shrugging its shoulders before throwing down the hood.

Nez nodded at her, raising his eyebrows. 'Cathy.'

Cathy punched him on the shoulder. 'Prick.'

He let out a gust of breath which was as close as he ever got to laughing. 'You came.' He sounded surprised.

'Don't sound so surprised,' said Cathy. 'I didn't plan on leaving you here all night.'

'No,' said Nez dryly. 'Just most of it. I thought you might have dozed off until the morning.'

'If I had, I would have lost my job.' She climbed out of the car and began wrestling with her bag to loosen it from under the seat.

Nez tutted at her.

'You should find something less stressful to do. Like gardening. Maybe you could write for a gardening magazine. How would that be?'

Cathy whipped her hair out of her eyes and slid a notepad and pen into her front pocket. 'If you know of any flower stories that can make national news, I'm all ears.'

Nez yawned, ignoring her.

'You will have to be quick in there,' he said, looking at his watch and glancing at his van parked over by a cabin with the lights on. 'I don't want this to attract attention.'

'Tell that to my editor.'

Nez looked around the area as if expecting journalists to jump out at any moment. 'He knows you're here?'

Cathy snorted, 'I bloody well hope not.'

Nez looked at his phone rather than putting the energy into replying. She was relieved; witty banter at this hour could only be maintained for so long. He turned towards the hill, putting it in her sights for the first time.

'I've got Charlie working on getting some more supplies, he's just popped into town,' said Nez, who had his arm inside a bag. 'This should be enough for a single trip.' He found some boots and handed them over for her to wriggle into.

'Come on,' he said, grunting at her. 'There's still time to get your story. It's good that you came early, the police will be here very soon.'

'You've called them already?'

'No, just wanted you to get a move on.'

They made their way up the hill after Cathy had zipped on a jacket and wriggled into a hat and gloves. He jerked his head towards the direction of the barn, his eyes rubbed-red from lack of sleep. He looked every bit as overworked as she felt. His pert lips broke into a grimace as he pointed towards the barn door and beckoned her closer.

Squelch, squelch.

The birds, not content to watch from the trees, flew ahead to land on the weathervane above the barn door which rattled in the wind as the two of them approached. Cathy had been in many abandoned and worn-out dumps in her time working local news, but even so, the look of the barn made her shiver.

'Can I get a quick interview first?' asked Cathy, who was starting to get nervous about the possibility of police arriving. She didn't want to lose Nez once the METs showed up.

Nez replied with a *do-you-have-to* stare.

'It will only take a second,' she raced to the cleft of the hill. 'Just tell me what happened.' She positioned herself a few steps down the hill and asked Nez to stand in front of the barn door with the sunrise breaking over the hilltop. 'Say your name, job and what happened,' she asked him, kneeling down and getting her camera ready. He stood in his dirty overalls and squinted as his long hair swept back in a gust of wind.

She hit the shutter release.

'My name's Nezahualcoyotl Maseualli...' he trailed off for a moment. Mercifully, Nez had spelled the name for her the first time they met. 'I'm from British Mexico. I run a chemical cleaning company and sometimes work for the council.' He slanted his body sideways and pointed back towards the barn. 'They said the farmstead needed cleaning. Old man passed away. Didn't say nothing about the barn.' He gestured towards the farmhouse. 'While cleaning, I heard sounds coming from inside. I took a peek...' He shook his head, running his fingers through his hair. 'I found at least a dozen dead. They're too starved to move. Lots are already rottin'. Been there three weeks—maybe four?' He teetered on the edge of his sentence, then glanced up at her. 'I called the police as soon as I found them.' She waited for him to go on. 'That's it,' he added, folding his arms.

Cathy pressed the pause button and reviewed the footage, holding up a hand to make him wait. She plugged a memory uploader into her head to extract the memory when she was done. Originals could be worth a lot, but until memory became replicable instead of just transferable, they still had their cameras.

'Could you…' she waved her hands a bit, 'talk a bit more about your reaction to finding the dogs. You know, how it made you feel.'

'Ah…' Nez continued, 'it was…' he made a face. 'Sad. A lot of them are dead.'

'What do you think of the owner?' asked Cathy.

The question confused him.

'What?'

'The person responsible, what would you say to him?' asked Cathy, hoping he would take the hint.

'I don't know him.'

Cathy breathed a heavy sigh and ploughed her fingers into her tired eyes to give them a rub.

'Grotesque?' Cathy suggested. 'Atrocious? Hideous?'

'Yeah…' said Nez, after giving it some thought. 'Hideous, exactly.'

Cathy smashed out the headline on the top of her notepad:

Dozen dogs found starved to death inside 'hideous' London barn

That would have to do, she thought, closing her camera and striding up to the top of the hill. Nez began zipping on his overalls and threw a spare outfit to Cathy, who tried to grab it and missed. The heavy-duty rubber uniform crumpled on the ground in front of her.

'You're gonna need that,' said Nez. 'They're too weak to try and escape, but they can bite well enough. I had to kick back a few last night. Lucky for us, seems as though they're used to it.'

Nez was a stone figure against the rust-red barn doors. His face was etched in a permanent frown as he walked around the side of the barn to his workers' truck and threw his keys on to the seat as he opened the door. He came back with a shovel.

'We might need this,' he told her, his lips refusing to allow even the hint of a smile. 'They won't take kindly to someone new.'

Cathy zipped on the saggy clothes and wrapped on her gloves. She felt warmer than she had all day. They stood there for a second, staring at each other, and suddenly Cathy wasn't so sure about all of this.

'Is it…' she stammered, 'how bad is…'

'Bad,' said Nez, without turning round. 'Not the worst I've seen, but bad. No people to clean up, at least. Lucky.'

'Okay,' said Cathy without hearing him. She was focusing on the sound that had begun to creep from underneath the barn door: A pining, high-pitched whimper, followed by heavy panting.

Nez passed her a flashlight after putting it on the lowest setting for her. It was cold and oily to the touch. 'You don't want to startle them,' he said. 'Make sure not to point it directly at them.'

She stood there with her camera, not knowing what to say.

Nez took a deep breath and slid the bolt back on the door.

'Ready?'

'Yes,' Cathy lied.

Nez wrenched the door open and she rushed inside, grasping her flashlight to stop it from rattling and hitting the on-switch.

Nothing happened.

'Nez, it's—'

The door swung shut, trapping her inside and leaving her in darkness. Cathy gasped as the smell hit her. She tripped, stumbling over something in front, and the torch fell tumbling out of her grip and smashed on the floor.

Crash.

The sound of broken glass echoed in the foul-smelling space.

She paused in mid-air, hand outstretched over the point where she had dropped the torch, unable to see or hear a thing.

There was a second of absolute stillness, just the sound of a tap trickling and water pattering on stone.

Then the growls started.

Yawing and yapping, chewing, slobbering, and the rustling noise of 20 hungry mutts sitting up echoed around the barn.

There was no barking, only a faint whine, pleading with her to stay. The growls curdled, growing fiercer, and suddenly howls emanated from the centre of the room.

The lip-licking sound of dogs hovering up their own saliva made its way to her ears, and she felt soft noses beginning to nudge at her ankles and fingers.

Cathy gasped and drew away, trembling as their wet, furry bodies brushed against her, licking her fingers, nipping at her ankles.

She cried out and jumped back, instantly regretting it as she inhaled the stench of a dozen dying, fur-covered bodies.

A deep, hungry growl came from behind her. The smell of damp fur filled her nostrils and she felt hot breath on her exposed skin.

Without thinking, Cathy picked up her camera from around her shoulders and pointed it towards where the centre of the growls.

The flash lit up the room.

Parched, black jelly rolled towards her in shrunken eye-sockets. The floor was coated with fur, matted with blood, mud, dogshit, saliva. Some had clearly been dead a while, rotted from the inside out, whereas others were starved. Skin was stretched drum-like over their bones; presenting shuffling, pink-black skeletons for her to record.

She set the camera off again with a *snap* and *c*aught a glimpse of a dog lying with its belly to the floor, head propped up on a haystack where it had died. Maggot-filled eyeholes stared up at her as the camera began to tremble. There were bloody bite marks on its side where the other dogs had started to nibble at it.

She forced her hands to steady and raised the camera again.

Snap.

Furless paws scrambled against the barn door.

Snap.

A dead mother lay strewn over soiled hay. Her pups were by her side, trying to nudge her over and extract what little milk remained in her dry teats.

Snap.

Mutts in the corner chewed on the remains of their dead cellmates, sucking the bones dry and slurping up the marrow inside. Hungry weaklings watched them with wide eyes, wondering when they would be next.

Snap.

Snap.

Snap…

She could only hold her breath for so long. Choking, unable to take anymore, Cathy cringed away.

20 pairs of black, shrunken eyes followed her around the barn, but most did not move. They were afraid, she saw in their eyes. Afraid of her Cathy found herself backed into a corner, unable to move or make a sound. She was petrified with fear—the only thing which was real to her was the smell; that awful, rancid stench that seeped its way inside, gagging, choking her as the mutts began to surround her feet. She felt a nip as one of them bit at her leg and cried out. Another one drew blood as it wrapped its maw around her wrist. She tripped, and suddenly they were all howling, bleating, thrashing as they surged forward, hundreds of yellow teeth closing around her.

She screamed.

Bang.

The door slid open and light burst into the room.

Nez was there, towering over the dogs. He snarled, swinging his shovel down with a crack and cutting open the head of the big dog holding Cathy. Blood trickled from behind its ear and it began stumbling, rasping and pining as it limped away before dashing behind a haystack.

Nez swung the spade into the side of the barn with a clang which made all the dogs scramble away at once. He showed his teeth before grabbing Cathy and heading for the exit.

Before Nez shoved her outside, Cathy looked back at the dogs. Most of them were still laying down. They looked weak and pitiful, all whimpering behind mounds of hay. Their eyes did not look feral and ravenous anymore, but hurt and afraid. Cathy stumbled back outside, and felt ashamed.

As soon as she was on level ground again, Cathy began coughing, retching the stink out of her mouth and heaving up dry phlegm as Nez swung the door behind her, sealing the dogs inside.

This is your big scoop, Cathy, she told herself as she let the camera swing around her neck. *Your big scoop at last.* The thoughts rang hollow. She should have been ecstatic, this was the biggest case of animal abuse in the history of the country, and she would be the one to break it. She did not feel ecstatic, though. She felt sick and tired—more tired than she had ever been before—and she wanted to go home.

She tried to get up and nearly fell again. Her heart was slamming into her chest, making her dizzy. Nez steadied her with his firm grip. She knew it was meant to comfort her, but with her racing heart, all it made her think of was how they didn't really know each other, and that nobody knew where she was or how to find her. Her heart felt like it might begin to wretch itself from out of her chest. She bit her lip, but it wouldn't stop trembling.

It's happening again.

She clasped her hands together and started rubbing them—trying to anchor herself to the feeling. Cathy pushed Nez away from her, trying to get to her car, but instead fell to the floor in a trembling mess.

He rushed to help her.

'No,' she gasped, digging her nails into her palms and rationing out her breath in long, shuddering rasps. Her heart rate raced out ahead of her breathing, and the panic came faster than ever.

Oh god, oh god, oh—

Blood began to quickly circulate from the in-betweens of her fingers to her legs as what felt like waves of tingling heat washed over her. She gasped as her heart contorted inside her chest, every muscle feeling as though it were pulled taut as a bowstring. Her throat closed up so that all she could do was choke, clutching at the air like a caught fish left to dry out by the shore.

This continued for another minute, while she shook on the ground. Then, eventually, it passed, and she could breathe again. Her fingers felt tingly and her mind felt numb.

It was only then that she realised Nez was by her side. He had been saying the same three words over and over again for some time now: 'It will pass, it will pass, it will pass…'

She shuddered, breath returning to her lungs. Her vision was blurred and she realised that drool had been leaking from her mouth. She spat, hoping to clear her jacket, but the saliva dribbled down her front.

Nez reached over and cleaned it up with his sleeve, then wiped her mouth, propping her up with his coat and exposing his bare arms to the cool morning breeze. She saw a smallpox vaccination mark on his shoulder, a circle of serrated flesh.

She slumped into him, sapped of energy. They stayed that way for God only knew how long. The birds sang to each other from the treetops and the sun began to poke its dreary head over the hilltop.

Sunrise, thought Cathy, half-asleep, *I need to get up for work*.

'Panic attack?' said Nez at last.

Cathy nodded.

'How could someone do that…' she began to choke again. Nez sat in front of her and took her hands in his.

'It's not your fault,' said Nez, looking into her eyes. 'And they have done nothing to deserve it, true. But without suffering, without sacrifice, happiness could not exist.' He held her gaze for a moment. She slouched onto her side while Nez continued to talk. She focused on his voice and realised that her heart had slowed back to a normal level. He took her hands in his and began blowing air into it to warm them. Nez went into his bag and took out a med kit. It had a fresh bandage as well as some antiseptic inside. He beckoned for her to show him her bite. 'When Nanahuatzin descended to the underworld and sacrificed himself to sustain the earth, the other gods followed him, not because he forced them to, but because they were inspired by his sacrifice.'

Cathy, half-awake now, looked around for her notebook, fearful of missing good content. She had never heard Nez speak of his religion before, nor indicate that he had one.

'Many Tenochca think humans were created for the sole purpose of rejuvenating the gods through their offerings. Life would not exist without them, and so offerings must be brought to keep life sustained, else it will leak out of this world and return to Teotihuacan,' Nez continued as he treated her wrist. 'That cyclic system of creation, destruction and rebirth allows communication from the world of the creators to our world. Life, death, wet and dry seasons…all is explained in this way. Do you see where this thinking has led them? They see all as *nextlahualtin.* They do not understand that it is the self that must be offered, not the lives of innocents.'

Cathy's memory stirred. Nez was speaking of the Feast of the Flayed Men, a massacre that had occurred when Tenochca rebels had kidnapped 26 peacekeepers in revenge for the 2014 prohibition on teaching Nahuatl in schools. The POWs were painted in long red strips, given new names, and made to dance with the insurgents before they were seized by the hair and dragged to the top of the temples. Cathy remembered a news reporter reading out on TV that hair was taken from the tops of their heads—the site where their *tonalli* soul was said to reside—before their hearts were cut out and their bodies rolled down the steps to break at the bottom.

Footage had emerged weeks later when the rebels were killed or captured. It showed them preparing the flayed skin of the peacekeepers to be eaten in bowls filled with dry maize. Family members of the victims had watched some of the warriors still wearing the skins of their loved ones when the kidnappers were eventually captured. Cathy had been in her second year at university at the time, and was horrified when stories began emerging of attacks on Americans all over Britain and the Commonwealth in response. Most of the victims were either from the Mayan or Inca religions, instead of those of the Aztec. It was around that time the Birthright Citizenship Act was introduced.

She couldn't remember when Nez had stopped talking, but it must have been some time ago, because right then her memory-phone buzzed with a message from her editor.

See you at eight, it said.

She checked the time, it was 6:41 am.

Send the article, her sluggish brain jolted to life. *Jodie needs to see the copy, along with the photos.*

Cathy took out her notepad and began scribbling down her intro and following paragraphs in rough outline so she would have plenty of time to write up once they got back to the office. She looked back over her shorthand for Nez's quotes and squinted against the dim lighting, trying to penetrate through the symbols to remember their intended meaning. Half of it was scribbles and longhand, but she had enough to get a good quote. She began writing up the long version:

Police are investigating the disturbing torture and killing of six dogs in Hyde Heath, Buckinghamshire—ran the first paragraph. She hesitated on the second. *One council worker told* The Column *the deaths were the worst acts of animal cruelty they had ever seen*—she lifted her pen, frowning. Too mundane? She rewrote the sentence.

Vets found the pets crammed into pens starved and ankle-deep in their own faeces—A little better, she affirmed, but still unconvinced with the effort. Jodie would be pleased with the detail, but the angle wasn't quite right.

She made a third attempt.

Emergency services found the pets crammed into pens ankle-deep in their own faeces in what officials say may be the worst act of animal cruelty seen in the UK.

She shuffled back. Good, if a little long. It would do for now. She moved to the third paragraph:

Claws and body parts were discovered scattered across the site, along with a mound of dead pups.

Her hand started to shake as she wrote the last paragraph, but she soon steadied it and reviewed her work. Not bad. She quickly began to transcribe her shorthand and finished the rest of the story using the info Nez had sent her and second-hand reports about the farm from the council's last inspection.

She decided that Nez would be the first speaker. His deadpan, matter-of-fact way of explaining the situation would work well on paper. She attached the article and her photos and sent them off to Jodie.

'Come,' said Nez, putting his hand on her shoulder. This time she did not shy away, but let herself be let away from the soon-to-be crime scene. She looked over at him again while sliding her notebook back inside her bag, wondering if he was thinking about the dogs. 'Rest now,' said Nez. 'You've done all you can. Let your boss publish it, sleep for an hour, then when the police have arrived, you can talk to them.'

'I need to work,' mumbled Cathy, sleepily.

'No,' said Nez, opening the van door and waiting there, sternly, for her to enter.

She did, crawling over a bed cover and mattress until she found a comfortable spot. It smelled of him. She turned around to see him gazing at her from the car entrance. His frame was blocking the way out, and she could see his breath condensing in the freezing air and his chest rising and falling with each breath.

'Sleep,' he said, eyes frozen on her. 'I'll wake you soon.' He closed the door, shutting the morning light out. Cathy rolled over to sleep—setting an alarm for 50 minutes. That's how long it would take for the paramedics to get here, according to Nez, who had spoken to them a moment ago using her phone. There was nothing she could do until then. Nez had given her a blanket, and she found herself wedged in-between strong-smelling chemical tankards. Before falling asleep, she quickly scribbled down what she could remember of Nez's story, then rolled over to bed. As slumber overcame her, she heard the rustling of crumpled paper, and shuffled back to find she was lying on a pile of receipts. She opened a nosey eye to take a peek, and saw that the most recent receipt was for a flight to Venezuela, flying first class on the previous Wednesday. *How had Nez been able to afford first class?* She wondered, as sleep-tainted thoughts washed over her. Before she fell asleep, many questions arose: such as when the police would arrive…and how the dogs had gotten there in the first place—but before any of them could take hold, she nodded off to sleep.

***

Cathy woke up to the sound of car engines, latex gloves being snapped on to wrists and middle-aged men shouting orders. She saw flashing lights outside the car window and began to panic as soon as she realised she had overslept. She looked at her phone. Five hours had gone by. She had six missed calls and a dozen messages from Jodie.

Shit.

Cathy grabbed her camera, notepad and pen, then jumped out of the van to corner and interview the first person she could find. The smell hit her for the second time that day, overpowering her senses and shaking her awake. The barn had become a hive of activity over the morning. Vets were carrying the dogs out of the barn in slings and stretchers. A trail of dark, limping animals could be seen stretching back to the RSPCA vehicles.

'We got a call in from about 8am from a worker set to clean the building,' said one of the staff she had cornered, whose name was Eddie. 'We were told that the dogs had been left for days, maybe weeks and that a dozen were dead already. We thought he must be exaggerating…we barely had enough RSPCA guys to get them all out.' Cathy nodded as she scribbled down every word, urging the man to go on. 'They're barely able to move. Most won't make it through the day.' He shook his head. 'People have been saying that the guy who the barn belongs to owns a race track. He got a licence to train them for the races, but nobody had been checking on them.' He paused and glanced at the rest of his crew. 'I don't think I'm supposed to be telling you this. Don't tell Frank I said anything.' He hurried back to work.

Cathy worked her way around the hill, stopping as many vets and RSPCA employees as she could who looked as though they had a spare second, and snapping her camera at every available opportunity. Cathy had learned that if you talked to someone enough, they started to assume that you liked them and were then more likely to tell you things. What you were saying did not necessarily have to be valuable, but the thought that it might be worth something made the other party feel obliged to you in return. For example, while Nez was busy talking to the paramedics and coordinating with the RSPCA, Cathy had decided to befriend the boy called Charlie who worked for Nez's company.

'I started out just chicken-pickin',' Cathy scribbled away as Charlie shrugged his shoulders and chewed out his words. He was sitting on the fence surrounding the barn, bouncing up and down on his hands as he got more excited. 'You get an apron, a pair of gloves and a bag. Every chicken you grab and shove into the bag gets you a quid. I once got 23 in one sitting,' his head bobbed and a droopy smile spread sideways as he remembered the moment.

'23?' awed Cathy. 'That's incredible.'

'You bet,' he giggled like a toddler stomping on sand castles. 'Easy to get the knack of it growing up with 'em, you know?' He had a wispy beard, undercutting a short chin where blooming mutton-chops were looking to meet in the middle. 'Uncle Isaac said I was getting so many he wanted me to come and work in the city full time, said I had a career ahead of me in coordination if I had my wits about me. I worked there for nearly two full weeks.' His head drooped for the first time since he began talking. 'I enjoyed it at first—kept going up to uncle Isaac and thanking him for givin' me a chance, said I wouldn't let him down. But I kept forgetting stuff. Easy things, you know? They'd explain how something worked and I would nod along and say I got it—and sometimes, I really did get it—but then after I got to working again, I'd forget it all, and it didn't make sense anymore.' He hung his head as Cathy kept scribbling, hoping he was on his way to talking about the dogs. 'Halfway through the second week, uncle Isaac comes up to me and says, "You know what, Charlie, maybe this just isn't your cup 'o' tea," and I pretended to look all sad like it meant a lot, 'cus I knew it meant a lot to him. But really I was glad. Uncle Isaac took me back to the barn after that, and I started chicken-pickin' again.' He looked at his shoes for a moment. 'That was about 16 weeks ago. What happened after is a blur. One day Nez comes to the barn. He's speaking in that funny, *Naarr-waatt* language he talks in sometimes…thought it was the strangest thing I ever heard. I know he's from the city. I'm used to getting ignored a lot, you see? But then he asks if I could come out and help deal with a few chicks for him. I say alright, I've been catching 'em all day, few more couldn't hurt. That's when he takes me out back and shows me a group of little 'uns. They're all suckling at their mum. Usually it's only the grown-up ones I gotta deal with—no point in plucking little 'uns when there's no meat on 'em. "You sure?" I ask him, and he says he is, so I reach down and I start wringing 'em.' Charlie twisted his hands in Chinese-burn twists, once, twice, and a third time. 'Like that,' he said. 'Then he says "good", and asks me to do the mum as well. I look down and shrug and say "okay". 'Cus what's one more, you know?' He paused for breath, letting out a quiet sigh. 'After that, Nez said he'd have me. We've been on the road ever since.'

Cathy looked up from scribbling. 'Do you enjoy it?'

Charlie didn't hesitate. 'Best time of my life,' he said. 'Always something new, never get the same day twice. First it was tough—seeing all 'em people and that, now I just love it. We were in Bristol for a double om-ni-cide last week, in Cardiff for a smelling basement the week before that. Now this.' He smiled gleefully at the sight of the vets and RSPCA hazmat wearers coming in and out of the barn, bundles of fur tied up on stretchers. 'It's something innit.'

Cathy had to agree. She had just about enough for a background feature—starting with Nez, moving on to Charlie and then the paramedics and RSPCA members—and she could pitch it to Jodie as soon as she was back in the office. She asked Charlie if he would pose for a photo, which he was more than happy to do. That droopy doctors-office grin would stay with her over the next couple of hours as more and more emergency services began to arrive.

She took a moment to watch the paramedics and RSPCA carrying the dogs in bags of matted fur, looking not half so terrifying in the daylight as they had in the dark. So thought of something Nez had told her after she asked him about the clean ups.

The worst is the dogs, he had said, while they shared a cigarette outside the courthouse. *People who kill themselves usually forget about the dogs. Dogs get awful peckish when they're locked up. And the worst part is other family members often don't want them after. They're too much of a reminder.*

What happens to them? she remembered asking.

Nez had stamped out the cigarette. *In all honesty? It depends how busy a day we're having.*

Speaking of the devil—of thinking of him, rather—Nez emerged from the barn for a third time, looking tense. Cathy supposed the stress might finally be getting to him. Charlie mumbled something about checking on the van, and left her alone. Cathy was watching Nez and barely heard him. He walked out of the barn, pushing his way past sweaty paramedics and grimacing vets until he was blinking in the sunlight, back to the grassy hill. He peeled his facemask off and began to strip out of his overalls. A thin line between the brows divided his forehead in two. His hair was long and straight, spilling down his shoulders and resting there. He was covered in shit, grime and blood, yet he did his best to maintain as much elegance as possible. He snatched a water bottle the paramedics had brought and emptied it in a single, long gulp. Nobody asked who he was or what he was doing. His was the type of confidence people didn't question. Cathy wondered if she had enough detail written to start a feature on him after the breaking news had subsided for the day. She began to scribble a few notes while he gulped down the water. After a few moments, she had something resembling an intro:

Nez Maseualli stood in the sun, working out how many chemical-resistant gloves he would need to detox the barn holding seven dogs still alive. He was 29, Tenochcan, and no longer ties his hair back before exposing himself to toxic fumes.

She looked up for a moment to watch Nez again before he disappeared back inside. He was looking at his watch and rearranging things in the back of the van like a car-park squatter who had spotted the ticket-inspector. Cathy continued with her drop intro:

UK law dictates that a facemask, goggles and overalls be worn at all times to prevent the sodium hydrochloride from melting through the user's skin. The vets, paramedics and RSPCA had already dragged-out half of the canines showing signs of life. The rest were left behind to rot. They would be Nez's job to clean-up.

Nez had brought with him 16 jugs of sodium hydrochloride, along with 21 pairs of gloves, inside an inherited van. He estimated he would use at least half-a-dozen of each before the day was over. From 1997 to 2012, Nez's uncle, Eztli Maseualli, had lived inside that same van, sleeping next to enough toxic chemicals to decompose a dozen corpses. He had remained on the outskirts of London and was able to get a leg-up over his competitors by being on-call 24/7 whenever the detox company was needed. In the 15 years since he started the company, Eztli regularly cleaned up abandoned meth-labs, the bedrooms of teenage suicides and every kind of animal infestation. The worst part, he had told Nez before he took over the business years later, was getting payment from bereaved family members. Widows rarely want to spend their dowry money cleaning up their husband's remains. This was a lesson which would serve Nez well when he first travelled to the UK in search of his sister, only to discover her murdered months later…

Cathy looked up from her pen to see how she was progressing. Jodie did not approve of drop intros; *this is not the New Yorker*, he would tell her, which was why she planned to pitch the story to at least a half-dozen nationals as soon as she got home. Everything could be checked over later with Nez in due time. Everything apart from the bit about his sister, who he refused to discuss.

A whistle was called once the majority of the dogs were out, and the rest were left in the barn because of the danger of moving them. The vets and RSPCA were called out and told to take a break. They would be back inside soon enough.

Nez noticed the two of them and whistled over to Charlie to bring in some equipment. Charlie jumped up immediately, running back to grab a bulky box-looking piece of equipment half the size of him. He carried it gingerly inside the barn where both he and Nez disappeared.

'Aren't they supposed to wait until after we're done getting the mutts out?' Cathy heard one RSPCA employee ask another. His colleague shrugged and got back to work as Cathy left the two of them standing there, leaving to investigate the rest of the area.

Two of the RSPA responders had rolled down their overalls and were sharing a cigarette. Nearby, two vets were busy showing each other something on their phones. It seemed almost normal. Suddenly, she heard the sound of cars pulling up to announce the arrival of the police. The MET pulled up behind the hill and trudged up the side towards the barn, bringing with them a police line to cut off access to the barn. Two officers ran past her, memory-cleaners swinging from their hips. They were already setting up a press-vantage point up on the hilltop overlooking the barn, where photographers and reporters would be able to get a view of the dogs being carried out by the RSPCA.

Cathy looked at her memory phone and saw a message from her editor about getting a quote from the police. Her stomach began to turn. She was already pushing her luck by being inside the police cordon. Bringing more attention to herself would not be a wise move.

She raised this objection with Jodie, who sent her back an angry message, telling her to get the damn quote.

Cathy sighed. The officers looked younger than her. The unfortunate rule with police is the less experience they had, the more likely they were to freak out when they saw a journalist. Generally, you only made their job harder. She kept that in mind when she strode up to the person who looked most like a police sergeant, shoved a notepad under his nose and said: 'Hi, Cathy Winters, deputy reporter for the Column.'

The officer stiffened. 'ID, please.'

Cathy produced it and he snatched it from her, glared at it and thrust it back into her hands. 'We're very busy today, miss, so if you could stay out of the vicinity, we would—'

'Anybody been arrested yet?' she blurted, pen and paper in hand.

The officer frowned and started walking away, muttering about officers being unable to give comments.

He was no good.

She sidled up to the next most senior-looking officer, smiling, shaking his hand, and asking him if anyone had been arrested. Oh, and she was a reporter, in case she forgot to mention.

'Errr…' the officer fumbled for a moment. 'I can't tell you that…but I can tell you that people are in custody.' The officer folded his arms at her, looking pleased with himself.

That would be a yes, then, thought Cathy, scribbling down what he had said and walking away.

She paused to look over her shoulder to scribble down the name written on his badge, then walked away from the police line as his superior sidled down to have a quiet word about talking to journalists.

Cathy sent the news to her editor and awaited further instruction.

'You seem to be hard at work.' Nez dropped himself down next to her, smeared with dog shit and sweaty as any Brit in summer.

'Not as much as you, by the looks of things,' Cathy retorted, eerily aware that their chatter resembled that of a couple on a camping trip. It was easy to forget that this was his day job. He was a professional, just like her, Cathy had to remind herself.

'Charlie has it covered at the moment,' said Nez, wiping sweat from his brow. 'There's not much more to be done until they get the last of the dogs out. That could take a while.'

Cathy scribbled down his quotes in shorthand, taking care to check her watch and write down the time of utterance. She sent the quote to her boss for an update.

'You never stop writing, do you?'

Nez was squinting at her with an expression just short of a smile.

'Well, you know,' Cathy said, hiding her notes and pretending to be checking for something in her bag. 'Never a dull moment.'

'What were you writing about before?' asked Nez, noticing her coyness. 'You seemed pretty preoccupied with it.'

Cathy thought for a moment. 'About you,' she replied, cautiously.

Nez considered this for a moment.

'Am I really that interesting?' he asked. 'You would think there are more fascinating stories about today than the life of a glorified cleaner.'

Cathy shrugged. 'People will want to know who it is that found the dogs. You're in the middle of what's happening here, and people naturally need a figure they can relate to. Nobody knows anything about the circumstances and the owner seems to have left the country.'

Nez snorted. 'Why are you so certain of that? The day is not over quite yet.'

Cathy could see the rest of the press lining up outside the police cordon and felt a wave of gratitude.

'It could be something that never gets solved,' said Cathy, pondering. 'Like the Zodiac killer or the Astronomy murders in the 80s. One time, I was writing a piece on this Welshman who killed his wife and then ate her...'

Nez was no longer listening. His attention had turned towards the sound of squelching boots and a heaving gut brought the officer standing behind them.

'Excuse me, miss,' it was the sergeant who Cathy had been talking to earlier. 'We've set up a press line outside the police cordon over by the trees there. I'd like you to go join the rest of the reporters out there, please.'

Cathy opened her mouth to protest but not before Nez had stood up and placed himself between her and the sergeant.

'Sorry, officer,' Nez began, in that non-pulsed and casual manner which he seemed to turn on and off. 'I think there's been a mistake. Cathy isn't part of the press; she's part of my team.'

The sergeant looked from Cathy, then back to Nez again.

'That so?' He asked, quite rhetorically. 'Well, she's been talking to my unit, who are on duty. They're very busy and need to work without any interference from the press. She'll have to join her colleagues over at the vantage point, I'm afraid.'

Nez did not seem to agree. 'Not possible,' he shook his head. 'She's vital for our role to complete the detox process, we need documented evidence of everything we do. Unless you want to pay for the clean-up yourselves...got the budget for that, do you?' he let the threat hang in the air.

'Right, that's it,' said the sergeant. 'You're going as well—come on,' he gestured for both of them to move behind the parameter.

Nez exploded.

'What the *fuck* do you mean?' he was shouting now. The *ck* had a hard K, typical of new world accents, which made the remark hiss in the air long after it had been uttered.

'Calm down,' said the officer, coolly. 'I've just asked you to move behind the police line until the operations are finished. You can come back after to finish the clean-up.'

Nez called the officer a cunt.

'Right, you've had your chance. Move back.' The sergeant put his hand on Nez's chest, pushing him and lowering his other towards the taser at his belt.

Nez didn't budge.

'I said move back.'

'Nez,' Cathy tried to get his attention as he seethed. 'Nez—It's fine—look, it's fine. I can go back to the vantage point, this isn't worth it.'

It was clique, but it seemed to work.

Nez hissed and started muttering in Nahuatl, turning away from the sergeant and striding off towards his car. Cathy looked at the sergeant with an apologetic glance, but he was too busy frowning at the other reporters who had been taking photos the whole time and stormed off in a huff himself. He waved at the other officers not to follow them. Cathy ran after Nez to drive around the hill before they were both escorted away from the farmyard.

'The police sergeant,' Cathy said, stirring as they drove away from the barn and tried to find a way in through the back entrance. 'I have footage of him pushing you back. I can send it to my paper.'

Nez was quiet for a moment.

'I would rather that you did not,' came his reply.

Cathy was not about to let it go. 'He pushed you, that's assault. You were legally allowed to be there. He had no right to treat you that way. I'm going to file a complaint.'

His response was calm and stony-faced.

'No.'

They were silent for a single minute or two until the silence became unbearable and Cathy opened her mouth to say something, but not before Nez spoke first.

'I have made my peace with—'

He was interrupted by the sound of ambulance sirens booming from the back entrance. The vehicles were jamming the road all the way back to the gate. There was a crowd of reporters and curious passers-by standing behind a police cordon which had now been stretched around the entire farmhouse and blocking the entrance.

'Something's happened…' Cathy muttered, wrenching the door-handle open as soon as Nez pulled up next to the fence and swung her camera over her shoulder.

She left Nez behind, racing up to the crowd and trying to push her way through a gang of photographers. A tall police officer was holding the crowd at bay with a calm expression and two officers flanking him at either side. She could see their eyes jerking towards her camera then back at her face, their expressions hardening as they put two and two together.

'This area is closed to the press, miss, we…'

'I'm with Nezahualcoyotl,' she said, clinging her notepad to her chest like a lifeline. 'With the detox crew, we were inside the barn this morning.'

The tall officer shrugged. 'I can't let you in, I'm afraid. You'll have to move on.'

'But—'

'Sorry, miss, I said you'll have to move on.' He turned away from her. Cathy slumped away from the police cordon and towards the back of the queue, where the other reporters were clamouring for a photo of the emerging ambulance crews. She hated pile ups.

Nez's face appeared in the crowd.

'Charlie is inside,' he shouted over the din, his face etched out of concern. 'He says he can get me back in. I have to go, Cathy.'

She urged him on, moved by the look of extreme worry that had come over his usually calm features. 'Of course, make sure he's okay.'

He disappeared into the crowd.

Cathy felt a buzz in her pocket. Her editor was calling her.

She opened her eye-drops bottle and splashed it into her streaming face before picking up.

'Interview?' was the first thing he said.

Her hands started to tremble.

'I'm talking with the police chief in two minutes,' lied Cathy. 'He's still inside talking with the vets.'

She heard Jodie swear and the sound of something breaking, probably a pencil.

'The Daily had an interview with the head vet go up ten minutes ago. Why do they have that and you don't?'

His voice tunnelled all the way down through her ear and out the other side.

'My interview will be more in-depth,' said Cathy, tensing from the force of keeping her voice from wavering. 'He's been more involved with the animals and the crime scene; he'll have more to say.' She clenched her teeth as she waited for his reply.

'He better,' warned Jodie. 'Just don't be late, okay? Whatever you do.'

'I won't,' her voice was going hoarse.

'We're getting the lead tonight,' he went on, expanding into a ravenous rant, 'I can feel it.'

'Of course we will,' said Cathy, her voice on automatic as she hurried away from her car and back to the police cordon. She had no idea what he was talking about.

'There's a lot of buzz on the wires, all the big-name papers will be there in a few minutes. I've sent James and Michael down too.'

Okay, she was not sure if she said the words aloud or in her head.

'And Cathy,' he paused, chewing over his words. 'Good work.'

He hung up before she had time to acknowledge the compliment. Her heart pounded in her chest as soon as she realised he had thanked her, two words she had never expected to come out of her editor's mouth.

That's when she left—walking away from the fence, from the crowd and from everything.

She ran back to her car.

Think, Cathy, *think.*

The notebook in her hands had started to shake by the time she had reached the bottom of the slope. Keep it together. She was limping by the time she got to the top and storm clouds had started gathering above, while a surge of thunder could be heard echoing from between the whirl of police sirens in the distance. You can figure this out, figure it out.

But there was nothing to figure out. The paramedics were gone and any footage or quotes they might have offered had gone with them. The story would break every headline, be on every news station in the world—and she had missed it. In the morning, no one would remember who sent the first photos, who had the first exclusive. The news team would only remember that she had let the story of a decade slip through her fingers. She would be fired, and she had run out of money and connections, knowing that any story could be her last. She had gambled everything on getting her scoop when she set out with her flatmate's car this morning. She had lost. Cathy hoisted her backpack a little higher, feeling the weight of its contents strain her lower-back and knew there was nothing for it.

The car was now in sight. It was time to go home.

She heard a muffled voice carry over the stunted hedges. A kid's voice. It was counting.

'9094…'

The birds had stopped chattering and now only the trees were singing, the wind rustling through their dead leaves.

'9095…''

She rounded the next corner, drying the corners of her eye.

'9096…'

Cathy blinked. It was Charlie. He was looking up at the sky, counting something. She looked up to see what he was looking at. It was the middle of the day.

'There you are,' he said, his head bobbing up and down like a yo-yo. He had that simple, dewy grin, except this time his eyes were narrow, slits cut into a ball of flesh balancing on two shoulders.

She wiped her eyes on the back of her hand before he could see.

'Charlie?' she asked, wondering if he had come to ask her about the interview. 'What are you doing here? Doesn't Nez need your help?'

He started at her for a moment, smiling. His hair was coated with sweat and he was breathing heavily as though he had run here. Although he appeared the same, he stood taller. He was looking her in the eye, which he had avoided before, and his irises gleamed with an intense curiosity. She took a step back, unnerved.

He held out his hand.

'I need to give you this.'

Cathy stared at him. He was holding a memory uploader.

'Whose is it?'

'Better not to ask,' he said, holding her gaze while they spoke. She was alarmed at how calm he looked. When she had interviewed him, he had barely been able to sit still, not daring once to look at her. Now his eyes had nowhere else to look. They were full and black, taking up his whole face. Like a dog's eyes.

She reached out and took it, feeling the weight of the cool plastic in her palm.

Charlie grinned at her, beaming as though she had been the victim of some nasty prank about to be revealed.

She wanted to question him more, her worries forgotten, to find out what trouble she was getting herself into. But Charlie turned to go.

'Wait,' she asked him as he finally broke eye contact and began to leave. 'What happened inside? Did you hear what happened?'

He paused, raising his head as though listening to the birds and the sound of the trees. 'Take a look at that memory and you'll find out.'

He disappeared off down the hill, whistling to himself. Cathy hesitated with the uploader in her hand, knowing she was about to break every rule in the book. In her bag lay a copy of the IPSO guidelines, which specifically stated that a journalist must have written consent from the individual, signed by both parties and with an independent witness, before using an uploader for a story. The only caveat to the rule was if the memory could be argued to be in the public interest, something she would need to have *prima facie* evidence of, and did not. She swallowed, feeling Jodie's breath down her neck and the threat of losing her job in front of her. She knew reporters who had been sued by their own newspapers for less.

Privacy laws were made to be broken, she decided, jamming the metal into her head and pressing upload. The memories hit her like a freight train.

***

Only a couple of hours after they found it and the barn didn't look so bad after all. Well, apart from all the dead dogs that is, thought Eddie. But, at least, he wasn't being barked at and scratched all day now; you need to look on the bright side of things sometimes.

They worked in pairs. Carrying the dogs out in bags one at a time. One person held the bag, the other loaded the corpses into the open bag so that it could be sealed and taken outside. Every now and then, bossman Frank would wander in to see how they were getting on, then he'd go and clap them all on the back and say something along the lines of "good work boys" and "almost done lads" and they'd say something slightly cheerful back at him and then maybe they'd smile for a few seconds till they got to the next bag and the smile would slide right off their faces again. At least Frank was trying though, you had to give him that. He even said Hi to the RSPCA guys that he didn't even know, even to Eddie.

One of the younger workers had started scrubbing the floors. They had been a dark shade of brown which was now smudging back into a dark red. Eddie thought his name was Charlie? Normally nobody cleaned up after the animals, so it was hard to tell. Eddie thought he should thank the boy before they both went home. He had done a lot of work for one day.

There were about a dozen police cars outside, they'd even had a news helicopter flying over this place about an hour ago. They were having a hard enough time trying to keep reporters outside from getting through the gate.

While working, Eddie found an envelope on the floor, addressed to someone called Michael Crotter. On the front of it was a house address: 17 Patterfield Lane, Slough. He walked over and handed it to Mark, the officer on duty.

'Cheers Ed, we'll send it down to evidence.'

'Been there yet?' asked Eddie, pointing to the address.

Mark nodded. 'We got a couple of the guys up there now.'

Eddie said thanks and got back to work.

There were about six of them in the barn still, they were almost done here. They all worked in silence. It used to be the kind of job that made for good banter, but since Simon and Danny had left, it had all dried up. He wished they were back.

Eddie was lost in his own thoughts when he caught movement under the corner of his eye. He looked around but saw nothing.

But he could have sworn he saw…? No, no, it had been nothing, they'd already taken out all the live ones.

He went back to work.

That was when he heard a faint cry.

He turned around, did it come from over there?

Eddie heard it again.

Something was moving under a moth-eaten blanket in the corner of the barn, somewhere nobody had checked yet— nobody had needed to, there hadn't been any cages there— but Eddie had heard something. He walked over to the corner and stood under the dull blue blanket. It moved, and then started to cry.

They all heard it this time.

'What the hell was that?' asked Frank, looking around.

Eddie was standing over the blue, moth-eaten blanket, white as a sheet. Pink fingers wrapped around his large fist. 'Guys,' he said in a high-pitched voice that raised the hair on their necks. 'Guys, there's a fucking baby in this blanket.'

***

Cathy took a gasp of fresh air and snatched hold of the uploader as it came to an end, staggering from the mental exhaustion it had cost her. After a few deep breaths to calm down, she realised what she had just seen. Her eyes glazed over as she scrambled towards her car, grabbed the handle and put the keys in the ignition ready for take-off.

She quickly grabbed a pen and paper out of her car and scribbled down the address written on the letter from the memory:

Michael Crotter. 17 Patterfield Lane, Slough.

She wondered if the police were there already.

Before she drove away, she had another peek at the uploader, unable to believe that it was real, unable to believe what Charlie had given her. She stayed in the car and counted to three. On the last count, she fired up the engine, turned the car around, and then drove off with the uploader shaking in her hand.

***

The grand house loomed over her, aged by its modernness. It looked like a relic of the 2000s, with its glass-front facade, polished-stone patio and swimming pool backyard. It resembled one of Picasso's many early paintings, destroyed by the artist in his attempts to portray himself as infallible, the last survivor of its kind.

Cathy knew she was breaking one of the golden rules of her trade: Never chase a story without telling someone where you're going.

She saw a cat watching her from one of the houses as they walked towards the large building. The pet greeted her from the window by closing both of its eyes for a long moment in a warm cat-smile. Cathy beamed and closed her eyes back at it, having grown up with three cats and recognising the procedure. Seeing it reminded her of times by the fire in winter. Too bad it was inside, locked up and unpetable.

She arrived in front of the large house and positioned herself in front of the oaken door, a laughable anachronism compared with its modern concrete build. Cathy knocked three times. The knocks seemed to echo in spite of the small space, reverberating around the close they found themselves in and leaving Cathy feeling exposed. No one answered. It was locked.

'No good,' she muttered to herself. 'No sign of police.'

She took some photos of the house before leaving. A row of houses lined up in front of her, each polished door-knocker looking less appealing than the last. These were the kind of houses where she used to hate when death-knocking. Vulnerable people were the most frightening to her.

She walked up to house number 48 and rat-tat-tatted on the doorknob, swinging her right knuckle under her and putting her weight into it so it would echo all around the house.

No answer.

She moved on to the next house with an even bigger oaken door and a forest of pot plants astride the entrance. She listened, heard nothing, then went to knock again just as a large man with a bristly moustache opened the door and gaped at her.

'Hi,' Cathy beamed at him. 'I'm Cathy Winters, reporter from *The Column*—how are you?'

The middle-aged man made an outraged coughing noise and stuck a hand out to ward her off, as if she had come to his door with an outstretched handful of frogspawn. He mumbled something about "accosting" and shuffled his way back inside, eyeing her through the crystal window as he jolted the bolt back in place.

Cathy sighed and moved on to the next door.

Number 44, let's see what you've got.

It was a multi-windowed door frame with murky glass, making it difficult to see through. She hammered on the bottom right window hard enough to make the glass rattle.

She heard a noise, the shuffle of footsteps. Someone was talking to someone else. Floorboards creaked on the other side of the door and she felt herself being watched through the peephole. She waited with the utmost patience, doing her best to hide how drained and exhausted she felt.

Cathy heard a latch being removed and the sound of the door unbolted. She turned towards the sound, beaming.

'I'm—'

'You're the journalist?' said a tall lady, standing in the doorway with thick glasses and uncut hair. 'Yes, yes. I remember now.'

Cathy flattened out her pencil skirt, which she'd adorned in the car, feeling flattered at being identified by her appropriate profession. She offered her ID to the lady.

The woman huffed. 'Don't worry, dearie, I believe you. I thought they might send someone sooner or later. Only a matter of time, after Crotter went missing.'

Cathy shoved it back into her pocket and whipped out her notepad. 'Crotter? You mean number 48?'

'Unless there's some other Crotter family living nearby.' She folded her arms. 'Police was here a week ago after Mr Crotter went missing. You want to know what I thought of him, I suppose?'

Cathy tittered on one foot, dithering politely to try and disarm the lady. 'Well, his family don't seem to be very forthcoming.'

'They wouldn't be,' snorted the lady. 'Not that he ever sees them. I can probably tell you more about the fella than they can.' She looked guilty around as if to spot them listening in on their conversation behind a hedgerow. 'You aren't going to write that are you?'

'No,' lied Cathy, who stopped scribbling immediately and looked up at the lady.

The woman frowned at her, cobweb-wrinkles growing at the corner of her eyes. 'What do you want to know, dear?'

Cathy asked what her name was and if she would be willing to give her age. She made a rule of asking before she began taking notes—the lesson of ending many interviews with a refusal and having to explain to Jodie why she could not include that in the article. She also managed to get a photo after gesturing mournfully at her camera. Then she asked about the Crotter family and how long the lady—whose name was Alice Ackroyd, aged 77—had known them.

'Oh—about fourteen years?' she scratched her head, slanting her eyes and looking at nothing in particular. 'They moved over back when their youngest was only starting primary. He's about nineteen now.'

Alice had known about several properties that the Crotter family owned, but said they had never mentioned a farmhouse. They were a family of four: Crotter, his wife, and two kids.

'And the baby?' Catchy asked.

Alice said they didn't have a baby.

No pets, either. Michael Crotter was a corporate recruiter, who reportedly spent many months away from home. Why did he own a farmhouse, in that case?

'He was a serial adulterer,' said Alice, with no hesitation over spilling the beans. 'I don't care if Lucy knows about it, I've been telling her for years. That's why she doesn't talk to me anymore—I don't know if you can write that, but it's true.'

Cathy scribbled like a madwoman, jotting down every juicy drop.

'It's not good for her; being left alone for months at a time, the poor thing left to deal with the kids all on her own. It isn't good for a woman. God wouldn't blame her if she'd found someone else. Heavens, I barely see them talk anymore. Maybe he got wrapped up in something he shouldn't, my theory is he's run off with one of the junior partners he likes to recruit. You see if he hasn't.' She cackled, high off her own mirth. 'It will probably do the two of them some good—they were damn near sick of each other anyway.'

'Was he open about his affairs?' Cathy looked up from her notes. 'Every neighbourhood has rumours.'

Alice waved her hand from left to right. 'Ask anyone on this road,' she affirmed. 'Everyone knows about the Crotter family, alright. They're probably the most complicated family in this neck of the woods, and that's saying something.'

Something stirred in Cathy's memory. Family is always the most complicated.

'Did you ever hear of any, em…' she thought about how to phrase the question in a way which wouldn't lead to the paper being sued for libel. '…other immoral activities he might have been engaging in?'

Alice blew a raspberry and twirled a finger. 'If he was a little more discreet about it…I've no doubt he got hold of a little junk every now and again—but that comes with the territory, I suppose. You got anyone in your family with a sweet tooth, dear?'

Cathy, caught off guard, looked up from her shorthand to meet the tall lady's gaze. She bit her lip. 'My dad…he still uses.'

Alice's brow softened, but her eyes stayed hard like she had been expecting the answer. 'You still talk to him, dear?'

'No,' she replied.

Alice nodded.

'Good,' she said. 'My husband too.' She turned and spat on to the smooth-stone patio. 'Good riddance to anyone who brings that back to their family home.' She paused for a minute, looking at her hands, then back to the wall again. 'I hope the baby's alright.'

'I'm sorry?' said Cathy, unsure if she had heard correctly.

'I said,' said the old woman, nodding in the direction of the street. 'I hope everything turns out alright. He's leaving behind a good family, you know.'

'Right, yes.'

Cathy let her speak.

'Oh, yes, very good family. Been here since they were little.'

Something wet dripped onto the carpet.

'It's a pity about what happened to that family. I don't think he wanted to do it, not with the way he was. Poor things.'

'Yes. Do you know if—'

'Such a pity.'

Alice kept interrupting her.

'It's all their fault, you know. The cleaners. I heard them from behind the bushes when I was trimming the hedges.'

'The cleaner? Ms Ackroyd, I don't understand. What cleaner?'

She was nodding, encouraged by her confusion.

'He started working there about a few years back, very affable character, or so they would tell me. The Crotters never had a cleaner before, but this one was so helpful, so attentive. Another one started soon after, younger, they were always together. But then, one time late at night, while the Crotters were out, I heard something strange. The older man was crying, so I stayed silent. I heard the younger one come out to comfort the older, or so I thought, but then, I overheard what he was saying. And it was so awful. There were threats, about his family, about what would happen if they didn't "go through" with it. They would talk about forging records, and documents. I wish I had heard more. If I was you, I'd look more into that missy.'

Cathy started writing in her notepad, but then caught herself stared at the woman, her pen forgotten. Alice was staring at the floor with bulbous eyes, brows about to tie together into a bow knot. The wet thing dripped again. Cathy noticed that it was the woman's hair, coated in shampoo, slipping off the thick coily tufts and dripping blue foam on to

121

the carpet. The rest of her was dry, fully dressed and beaming at the doormat.

She's quite mad, thought Cathy. *She thinks she's met me before.*

'Of course,' she said, after she found her voice again. 'You're right…Sorry, I blanked for a moment there.'

Alice suddenly looked up at her, then beamed as though just noticing her for the first time. Cathy asked her for a phone number and address in case the newspaper wanted to contact her. She laughed.

'I don't have a phone, dear. I disconnected it years ago, and I don't watch the news anymore. It's not good for the mind.' She paused, looking out at the rest of the empty neighbourhood. 'If you or your newspaper want to talk to me again, you know where I live. I shan't be going anywhere. You take care of yourself dear.' Alice closed the door, leaving Cathy with far more questions than answers. She pocketed her notes and walked back to her car.

Cathy quickly wrote up the story in her back seat and sent the copy to Jodie. Her memory-phone started to ring and she went for it, thinking it was Jodie.

It was Nez.

'I'm sorry, Cathy,' Nez's voice buzzed in her ear as soon as she picked up. 'I don't think I can let you back in. I've done all I can with the bodies, they barely let me get in to do my job.'

'That's okay,' Cathy heard herself say in a quiet voice.

'I don't think you will see me again. It's about my sister. I need to get her body back to my family. It's already been too long. With all this, I might finally have enough to afford the ticket back. You understand, right?'

'Yes,' her voice was on automatic.

'I have to go. I'll need to talk with the police soon.'

'What did they say?' she asked desperately, her voice straining.

'I'm sorry, Cathy, I can't tell you.'

A bubble formed in her throat.

'I just,' a sob wobbled her voice, 'thought you might want to wait till the article's *published*.' Her voice cracked on the last word, going an octave too high and betraying her.

'You know I want to help you,' came the crackling reply. 'But I can do more good back inside. It is where I am needed.' She stared at the floor in teary-eyed defiance, hating him for feeling sorry for her. She took a step back to steady herself. Nez said: 'You have everything under control. Good luck with your story.'

He hung up the phone.

That's it? She wanted to scream at him, her face bunching up into a mesh of tears and veins. As soon as the phone was down, she slapped herself.

No story about Nez. No scoop on the Crotters. No in-depth investigative piece on the motives. And after all this, she still thought Nez might have liked her enough to see her again. But that, it had turned out, was silly.

Fucking amateur.

She clawed at her arms, drawing red. She screamed silently, so that only a whimpering squeak came out of her. She grabbed chunks of her dyed-red hair and shook back and forth. She let her arms fall to her sides and started walking back to her car.

It was time to go home.

There were a dozen messages on her phone by the time she was almost out of the city. From her editor, other reporters, her mum, from her friend whose car she had stolen. She ignored all of them.

It was almost dark by the time they got within sight of the city. Cathy was just putting the finishing touches in-between waiting in traffic, attaching the photographs from their scout-out of the country-houses and patched it through to Jodie, for all the good it would do her. Her previous photos had been number one on trending, after being stolen by at least a dozen newspapers including the Central Broadcast Corporation. Her editor had sent emails to every news outlet in copyright breach. They would soon reply with a £200 donation addressed to her editor, along with the response which had become typical of the industry: "we made every conceivable effort to contact the copyright holder but were unable to locate the owner. Please accept a formal apology along with a copy of our photo policy from our lawyer."

The message received from every outlet would be identical. The photo would be left on their websites just long enough to attract leading hits before it was taken down. The don't-sue-me bribe would be pocketed and the dispute forgotten. But right now, Cathy's inbox was filling up with almost a dozen messages a minute and she needed some time to think.

Speaking with Nez, Cathy had realised something. Once upon a time, she had been topper of her class, the best student in the year; the best by-lines, the best scoops, everything. Then, one morning, all of a sudden she was miserable. It had hit her so fast she was not quite sure what happened and she had been in shock ever since. She could not pinpoint when it had happened exactly, but ever since she had been looking around at everyone else and asking: wait a minute? Has this happened to everyone? Will it stay this way forever? Since that day, she had been living under the suspicion that most people were living in a kind of quiet desperation, unable to admit that they wanted anything at all—now she was sure of it.

She got a message from her editor when she arrived back at her flat.

'James has arrived on the scene,' it read. 'He will take care of the interview. Get some sleep. More work tomorrow.'

She closed her eyes and felt the day catching up with her. Passers-by were avoiding eye contact, as usual. The sun was still shining its last evening gleams, and Cathy was tired Her flat appeared around the corner, feeling as though she had last occupied it a decade ago. The burnt-face man nodded to her when she walked past, but she couldn't react. When Cathy let herself in and rolled over to sleep, she realised that the screaming had stopped from the block opposite.

She waited in her room, feeling the weight of the day begin to lift. Suddenly, she had a look at one of the articles pinned to her wall. It was a copy of the inquest transcript over the court case where she and Nez had first met, where she had gone to learn about how his sister had died. Abandoned by her lover. Atzi Maseualli was her name. Cathy thought about how she had died, about the businessman who had brought her here, and about Nez. She read over it and over it and over it again, until she was absolutely certain. Her thoughts that night were troubled not by the screaming echoing around the square but by the dogs that howled in her dreams.

***

Cathy woke up the next morning to a message from Jodie, telling her to get down to the police station straight away because someone had been arrested over the starvation scandal. It wasn't until she had breakfast and checked her trends that she realised her story had broken national news. Everyone was talking about it, from her flatmates to members of parliament to the postman who dropped off her mail. The recorded footage had been seen by millions of people worldwide and Cathy already had a few messages from recruiters telling her national papers were interested in an interview.

Cathy walked past the newspaper stand propped up against a corner shop window, the cashier smoking his way from a packet of camels halfway through the Saturday morning paper. *The Column* was on the middle right, along with the other red tops it shared the stand with. Above it were the broadsheets, hosting an array of headlines but all sporting the same photo: the picture of Mrs Crotter being led away by the police in hysterical tears as they departed the scene. Only the facts were reported, but the implication resounded in every article: Michael Crotter's wife had denied every allegation that the child had been a bastard of her husband's, or that she had done away with the baby out of spite, choosing to feed it to the dogs rather than let the child live in her household after her husband left her. She would face trial in the summer of next year after the appropriate evidence had been gathered. A

DNA test would have to wait until the husband could be found. If he was not present, the wife would have to stand trial alone. Not that it mattered. The whole of Britain had already declared her guilty.

Walking past her came a pair of lovers holding hands, feeling the need to do nothing other than enjoy each other's company. A freckled girl was led by the hand of a taller, thick-jawed boy who held out a lighter for her and whispered something in her ear. Cathy did not even feel a pang of envy strike her as they passed by, giggling to each other. Maybe yesterday had got to her more than she thought.

Michael Crotter's name had been all over every radio station, TV outlet and news desk. An international manhunt had started, but so far authorities suspected he had fled to Venezuela after police found bookings made on his card a week ago.

Cathay kept on walking to the police station, closing in on a final story she had to chase up before she could relax and tie things up in one tidy bundle.

It was 9am. Cathy had another six hours of sleep under her belt, the most she ever got, and was feeling as refreshed as a newly-cleaned cat. She went to the reception as soon as she arrived to ask about check-ins.

Nez had been taken to the police station this morning.

At first, Cathy thought they had picked up the wrong person. Nez was well-dressed and clean. His beard was trimmed, and he had found time to cut his hair, making him unrecognisable.

But for once, she had him at a disadvantage. Despite his new dress, there were permanent bags under his eyes. His nose and ears were an ugly red, rubbed raw from the cold and his lips were a long way from a smile.

His eyes widened when he saw her, brows jumping as though tugged by an invisible string.

'Cathy,' he embraced her as soon as she was close. Although she had been outside for most of the morning, his skin felt cool to the touch. She embraced him only briefly and then stepped back so he could look at her. 'I am guessing you heard…'

He gestured at the reception desk and let his hand fall to his side.

Cathy nodded, looking at the papers being shuffled and stapled by the heavily make-upped receptionist.

'I did,' she swept her hair back from her face. 'Do you have to go so soon?'

'No choice,' said Nez, who stepped up and grabbed the papers from the receptionist as soon as they were ready.

She passed him his passport back along with his proof of address. 'Thank you very much for your help today, sir. We'll follow up with contact details in Mexico if you need to change your statement. Enjoy your flight.'

Nez thanked her and shoved them into his rucksack.

'Walk with me,' he said to Cathy as he turned towards the station's exit. 'I still have an hour or so left.'

The double doors opened to the sound of buzzing traffic and the rustle of a plastic bag being carried down the road by a gentle breeze.

Cathy's hand slid into her pocket and unfolded a copy of today's newspaper. Nez's face was on the midsection, bleeding from a feature on the second page... Her feature.

Below the headline, which had replaced Cathy's version, read the words: Catherine Winters, reporter at *The Column*.

Nez plucked it from her hands and started to read.

'You made me sound much better,' he mused after skimming through a few lines. Cathy laughed.

'People tend not to get mad at you for making them sound smarter.' She beamed as his eyes lit up, jumping from paragraph to paragraph. After a few minutes, his eyes fell and it was clear he had reached the end. 'At least I will have something to show for this trip.'

They walked on in silence.

'Will you ever come back?' Cathy asked, unable to stop herself.

Nez snorted. 'I hope so. Maybe to start my own practice but I have a lot to take care of, you know that. Besides, I could do with staying out of trouble for a while, after the celebrity light you've cast me in.'

Cathy smirked and knocked into him on purpose. Nez shoved her away and they both walked on across London Bridge.

'What about you?' he asked her. 'Still don't fancy writing about gardens?'

Cathy snorted and told him they had offered her the full-time deputy editor position this morning, along with a pay rise.

'That's what you wanted, isn't it?'

'I don't think I'm going to accept,' she said, thinking as she talked. 'I'm starting to think maybe this isn't the right gig for me after all.' The birds were singing above them, just like the birds near the barn. Cathy wondered if they were the same ones, migrating after all the commotion. 'Who is going to take over the company?' asked Cathy, brushing down her jeans as they descended the steps.

'My cousin will do okay while I am gone,' said Nez, 'Atzi needs a proper funeral. She does not deserve to be buried in this country.'

'What about Charlie?'

His shoulder's bunched up.

'He's coming with me. Or rather, I'm coming with him. I don't have a choice in the matter. That's what we both agreed.'

'What do you mean by that?'

He ignored her, and so they walked on.

'Your parents,' Cathy began, stopping halfway across the bridge. 'What will you tell them?' She let Nez walk ahead of her before speaking again. 'Will you tell them Crotter was the reason she died?'

Nez stopped to look behind her, squinting at something over her shoulder.

'So you know?' he asked her.

She nodded.

'I know. I thought about it after the inquest. How she died, why you wanted it taken out of the paper, the baby being ineligible for citizenship. You tracked him down as soon as you got to this country, and got a job as a cleaner.'

He tilted his head.

'Do you know why I did that?'

She shook her head.

'I haven't figured that part out yet.'

They walked on.

'Too much is happening too fast,' Cathy blurted out. 'You know they already raised half a million online to care for the baby they found. I wonder if anyone is looking to adopt.'

'Someone rich and with a good heart, I hope,' said Nez, without looking at her. 'If she survives, that is.'

She. Cathy had not mentioned the baby was a girl. Neither had any of the news reports. No one apart from the doctors treating it would know.

'What did they want to talk to you about? The police?'

'Just what happened, same as I told you.'

'Nothing else?'

He hesitated.

'And about my sister. They wanted to know how she died, why I'm here...the whole story.'

'What did you tell them?'

'The truth. That she married that cunt too early and went to live the perfect life with him, not knowing she'd be his mistress. And when she got pregnant, he left her to die on the streets in childbirth. Funny how things work out, isn't it?'

Cathay looked at him, and in that moment his glinting eyes grew hard, and his figure tense, and she saw the imprints of fingernails pressed into his palms.

'What happened to Crotter?' she asked him, trying hard not to take a step back.

Behind his glinting eyes, she saw the twitch of a smile.

'Dogs get awful peckish when they're locked up.'

Cathy didn't know what to say, so she said nothing. They set foot over London Bridge, pigeons swirling over their heads as the red buses passed on their right. The taxi rank was in sight.

They hugged on the bridge. Cathy clung on tight and squeezed her eyes shut, wanting it to go on forever. Eventually, though, Nez pulled away.

'Let me know what happens,' he told her.

'Hm,' she replied. 'I might be a bit short on material with you gone.'

'Yes,' he said, avoiding her gaze. 'Luckily, you have already written your story.'

'There's always the next one.'

For the first time since Cathy had met him, Nez smiled openly and fully. 'Like what?' he asked. 'A story about an immigrant, who killed a businessman in revenge for his sister's death, then framed the man's wife for animal abuse, all so he could pass off his niece as a British-born citizen? Doesn't seem like an easy pitch to me.'

Cathy blinked at him. 'Maybe you're right,' she went on. 'Like I said, if there's anything worth writing about here, I'm sure the professionals will pick it up.'

'I admire your faith in the system,' said Nez, picking up his bag.

His taxi was here.

Nez went to turn and Cathy took his hand, wanting to think of something to keep him. Nez stood forward as the taxi beeped again, then kissed her before she could move away.

Cathy made a sound, surprised. But she didn't move away. It lasted only a few seconds and then the moment had passed. Nez was turning to go.

'Take care of yourself, Cathy. I hope we meet again.'

With that, he got in, the taxi disappearing among the London skyline, vanished. Cathy eased herself down from her tiptoes, got out her notepad, and started to write.

Humming Noise

They found the body twisted up deep within the mineshaft. It was laying against a pile of chipped rock and discarded pickaxes.

'We found Alex.'

Three officers circled around the corpse. The light fell on the man's face to illuminate a golf-ball sized hole where the uploader had detonated, leaving a bright-red crater on the side of his skull.

'Rookie,' Sandra beckoned for Ross to move closer. 'See if there's any trace memory left.' She shoved a probe into Ross' hands then jerked a thumb towards the corpse. 'You need the practice.'

Ross lifted the metal probe; a prickly feeling running down his spine as he inserted it into his fellow officer's head and heard it click into place. The body twitched as neurotransmitters began to secrete into what was left of his frontal lobe, tracing out neural pathways and detecting the memories imprinted there. The dead man's eyelids began to flutter, flapping as his short-term memory deposits were mapped out and recorded by the probe. After about a minute, the procedure was complete and a thumb-nail sized uploader popped out the side of the probe—ready for use.

Clive knelt next to him.

'Alright,' he said. 'I know you haven't used memory imports in the field before, but it's the same as when you'd use one in training, got me?' he continued.

'Yes, sir,' said Ross, holding his breath as he pushed the uploader into the memory-port embedded in his own skull.

'It'll feel strange at first.' Clive continued. 'Like you can't quite remember which memories are yours and which aren't. Officer Sanchez' memories are recent, meaning that they'll be strong. You might remember being physically hurt or even killed—ready?'

Ross nodded.

'Good.' Clive gave him a cheery clap on the shoulder. 'Try not to overthink it.' Ross gulped as he felt the memory-slot at the back of his skull start to tingle. 'Trust me, these things will save your life more times than you can count.'

He pressed the upload button.

For a second, nothing happened. Ross listened to the sound of water dripping somewhere onto the cavern, building a stalagmite that wouldn't be completed for thousands of years.

Just as he opened his mouth to ask them how long it usually took to kick in, his limbs started to shake. Ross threw out a leg to steady himself and instead of cavern-rock, his boot crunched into sand. When he looked up, the sun was in his eyes and he felt very dizzy. He tried to batter the light away like a swarm of midges but instead knocked his radio out of its shoulder strap. He lunged forwards to catch the falling device, embarrassed, and gasped when his hand plunged into cool water.

Ross paused, retracting his wet hand with trepidation. The light faded away to reveal his own reflection glaring back at him, kneeling over a lake with his knees pushing down into creamy sand. He blinked back at his own reflected face, dimly registering that his eye colour had changed to hazel-nut brown and that his skin was several shades darker. He picked himself up, not thinking to question how he had arrived at the lake, and walked up the sloping bank, forgetting all about the combat boots and visor he had been wearing a moment ago. He frowned up at the row of mud huts in front of him. Withered shrubs littered the edges of the lake, the only greenery for miles around. Past them, barren desert stretched far into the distance, broken up only by the odd mining town and long abandoned industrial facilities.

Standing tall against the horizon, huge marble walls enclosed an array or spiralling towers that scraped the underbellies of clouds as they passed by. Beside them, reams of black smog billowed out from featureless towers. His eyes continued to drift across the barren landscape until he heard chattering coming from behind the nearby shrubs. People started to move in and out of the mud huts, carrying fish and reeds from the lake in hand-woven baskets. Taking no notice of him, children ran unattended on the beach. A young girl of around eight splashed beside him in the water, laughing as she chased a young antelope that had decided to wash itself by the stream. Up the shore, he saw a pair of topless women washing clothes in the water, flinging their hair back as they talked and ringing damp cloth dry.

'Alex?'

Alex spun around, eyes wide with alarm as a short, dark-skinned woman approached him from one of the huts.

'Where have you been, my love?' she asked before Alex could react. 'Come! The friends I have been telling you about are finally here. I believe one of them is from your city, yes?'

Alex found himself being led by the hand across the beach, past the shrubs and jutting rocks and into a clearing where three men were standing in a circle conversing. They stiffened as Alex approached, seeing his uniform, but relaxing as they took notice of the woman accompanying him.

As he stepped into the clearing, an enormous headache overcame him—he doubled over from the pain and his ears were filled with a strange humming noise. Suddenly, after a few moments, the pain had disappeared as quickly as it had come and the humming noise along with it. He peered at the three men in the clearing.

'Damien is from your city,' explained Alex's companion. 'He has been a friend of the people here for a very long time.'

'A pleasure,' Damien extended his hand towards Alex.

'Is that right?' Alex found himself replying without much intending to. Then, involuntarily, he reached down and produced his badge. 'Officer Sanchez—state your citizen ID and occupation.'

Damien retracted his hand with an icy coolness, motioning for his two companions to relax. He opened his arms wide.

'I'm still searching for my occupation, as it happens,' he said with a warm smile. 'My friends and I are travellers, disenfranchised from the wider world. Life can be tough on the outside, often short and brutal—People will do anything to get their families into the city, as I'm sure you know.' Alex went stiff. He looked behind him, then around at the trees and then back to Damien. He was still smiling. 'Let me tell you

136

about myself,' he went on. 'I've been on a long journey to get here. I've played many parts in my time, you see. Soldier, cleaner, businessman, criminal, husband and wife...' he drifted off for a moment. 'I've forgotten many things about myself, about the world. So much has happened, you see? It becomes too much for one mind. Now I realise I am not supposed to understand it, merely to store it and to protect it in any way I can. It will be all that is left, once we are gone.' He nodded towards the woman beside Alex, who smiled back at him as though nothing were amiss. 'Back before all of this, I used to be like you. Very much like you, in fact. But I didn't appreciate giving up slithers of myself to live in a city. I made my fortune, not the first, mind you, and decided to continue my research away from prying eyes. I wanted to be whole, you see? I was put here for a purpose, a thousand-year purpose, close to its conclusion. But now, I need what the city has to offer. I need to get back to the city, to civilisation, using anybody I can. Has your friend shown you the work we've been doing at the old sisyphum facility around here? Fascinating stuff.'

Alex moved his hand instinctively towards his belt, then whipped his pistol out of its holster and pointed it towards the trio, taking two steps back and shouting commands.

'All three of you, get down on the ground and state your citizen identification numbers. Loud and clear, please, so I can find out your business here for myself.'

Damien glanced from left to right with weary black eyes. Then after careful consideration he raised his hands. 'Oh, I can tell you,' he said, eyes twitching up over Alex's shoulder then down again. 'But I would rather show you.'

Something heavy crunched into the back of Alex's head and he fell to the ground; faint chuckling came from the bushes. He blinked as a man with a thick scar running down one cheek stepped in front of the light, holding a rifle dripping with his own blood. The rifle came down again and knocked all the lights out of his head.

When he awoke, he was in a tunnel. He was being led by two men to a rust-coated table. Alex froze, on the table sat a mask. It had a probe embedded towards the back and a hole in the top. Next to the mask was a drill—its tip was wet. Next thing he knew, his head was being pinned down and the mask forced over it, throwing him into darkness. A humming noise began to emit from the mask and he felt something white hot piece the back of his head.

'Ross.'

A voice pierced through the humming sound.

Alex screamed, lashing out with his fists as the humming got louder and cried out in pain as his knuckles crunched into hard rock.

'Ross, can you hear me?'

The light became very bright again and he found himself standing upright.

'Ross!'

He blinked the light out of his eyes, staggering around the mine shaft and throwing his hands out to steady himself. He raised his fists and saw that they were torn and bruised. The cavern wall was glistening red where he had struck it.

'Easy there! We've got you—you're okay, lad, you're good.'

Clive was standing in front of him, holding him upright and shining a torch into his retinas.

'Pupils aren't too dilated…He should be coming around by now. You remember who we are, lad?'

He heaved great gulps of air into his lungs.

'I…' he couldn't stop shaking. 'I'm…'

'Do you remember your name?'

'Ross,' he swallowed, getting his breathing back under control. 'My name's Ross.' It took him a few moments to realise that the other two had been staring at him for some time.

'Good, good.' repeated Clive. 'You're an enforcement officer. This is your first field mission. We were looking for Officer Sanchez after his HUD started flat lining. He's over there.' Clive nodded towards the corpse. 'You volunteered to experience his last moments via a probe to help us identify the attacker.'

His mind felt cloudy. Had he volunteered? He couldn't remember.

'Do you remember anything?'

Ross took his gloves off and rubbed his sweaty palms together, shoving them under his nose to trigger his olfactory senses so that the flashbacks subsided for good.

'He was patrolling near the creek, talking to some of the locals when he got separated from his unit. He was ambushed and then taken down into the tunnels…' He trailed off for a second. 'I think they tried to steal his uploads using a makeshift probe. They had a mask.'

'And the attacker?' Clive tried to jog his memory. 'Did Alex get a good look at him?'

'His name's Damien,' said Ross as the images floated back to the top of his mind. 'There were at least four of them—I couldn't be sure if any more are down here.'

'Traffickers,' muttered Sandra, frowning.

'Aye.' Clive pointed towards the hole in the side of Alex's head. 'The mask must have triggered the defence-uploader, killing him.'

'Looks likely,' Sandra mused. 'There's been a huge sisyphum mining operation down here.' She glanced at Ross.

'Must've been digging for a while,' said Clive, swinging on his backpack and pointing his flashlight down the nearest tunnel.

'How many do you think are down here?'

The question from Sandra stopped Clive in his tracks. He paused, then turned around wearing an unreadable expression. 'Dozens, at least,' he said. 'Judging by the amount of rock they've chipped away, possibly hundreds.'

Sandra looked suddenly pale. 'I'll radio the medics to follow us in,' she finished.

'How many what?' asked Ross, feeling more confused than ever.

'She's talking about mules,' Clive cleared up for him. 'The people who live near here…it's likely the traffickers were using them to start a mining operation. Most traffickers need money so they can afford to pay their own way into the city, whether by their own body or someone else's. For that, they need mules; people. It's possible they've had their memories forcibly removed to be sold on the black market. The traffickers often don't have the technology to do it selectively like we do, so sometimes—if they're kind— they'll wipe out every memory left. We call it negging.'

'That's kind?'

'Better than the alternative.'

Ross stared at the floor while the other two slotted equipment into their packs and belts, wondering what it must feel like to have your memory sucked out of you.

'How many more mines are there across the country?'

Sandra shrugged.

'This is the third one this year, and could be the biggest. They started in Latin America, with immigrants and rough sleepers led there with the promise of an easier life. Decades ago, they found hundreds of them popping up all across the continent, all part of the same group. This year is the first we've heard of them this side of the pond.'

'Remember your training,' said Clive, approaching him and tilting his head upwards with a steady finger. 'You handled your first ride really well. I know your head's still spinning but we don't know how many mules are down here—we need you to keep your head in the game until we've found out. Think you can do that?'

Ross straightened up, 'Yes, sir.'

Clive smiled. It looked like old leather being stretched. 'Stay focused. You've done this job a hundred times, just never in your own body before.'

***

He smelt them before he heard them. The rancid stench of unwashed bodies, mixed with excrement and rotting meat seeped down the hallway under their visors and up their nostrils. Clive swirled his finger clockwise and made a sweeping motion, signalling them to put on their masks. They began to hear shuffling feet near the end of the tunnel. An animal-like bleating began to echo around the cavern as their flashlights lit up the hallway in front.

Ross raised his rifle, white knuckles clenching and unclenching the grip.

Remember your training, he told himself as the bleats turned into a collective grunting sound and Clive motioned for them to move up to the walls. *Remember your training.*

Suddenly, the mine shaft was covered in eyes.

They hid their faces as soon as the officers found them, throwing up their hands to protect their eyes while the flashlights illuminated their sun-parched skin. Some blinked with a fish-like slowness, their pupils refusing to dilate as the light streamed through their retinas—testament to the months they had spent away from the light. Others curled up into balls as soon as they approached, trying to cover up their skin, chequered black and blue with bruises.

A moan interrupted his steps and Ross looked down to see a face he recognised. It was the dark-skinned woman from the lake who had taken Alex to the clearing by the hand—she had called him love. She was gazing at Ross' flashlight listlessly, wearing torn cloth and a slack expression. In her hands, she was clutching a girl no older than eight—the same one who had been chasing the antelope by the shore. She looked as dazed as her mother. As Ross approached, she reached out towards the tip of his rifle with pale, stumpy fingers. He noticed that she had hazelnut brown eyes, the same colour as Alex. The mules gazed at the three officers with tentative wonder, shifting ever closer to their flashlights like moths drawn to a flame.

'What happened to them?' Ross was unable to stop looking at the face of the young girl, drooling on to Sandra's boots as she strapped a safety band around the girl's bruised arm, marking her as a priority for the medics. All of their hands were covered in blisters and scabs where the traffickers had made them chip away at the rock. 'It's like they don't even know we're here.'

'Their memories were sold,' Sandra told him through gritted teeth. 'Most of them come from rural communities, tricked into coming down here after being promised fair pay for a mining job. As soon as they're below the surface, zap! Negged—they're strapped onto a table and have every positive experience they've ever had sucked out of them to be sold on the black market.' She let go of the girl after securing her and watched as she slumped on to the cavern floor like a sack of potatoes. 'This is what's left of a person once everything else is taken away.'

Ross remembered the metal mask and shuddered.

Clive marched back towards them and scraped up something off the ground. He held it up towards the light, squinting. 'Another sisyphum uploader,' he announced. Clive brought it to his ear, then spat and threw it to the ground. 'It's been tampered with,' he said, looking at the pile of uploaders in disgust.

Ross picked one up and held it to his ear. 'It's humming' he said, gazing back at Clive and Sandra.

'That means it's been uploaded with fabricated memory,' Sandra explained, slapping arm bands on the last of the mules. 'They were likely using it to sedate the mules while they stole their positive memories to sell on the market—awful kind of them.'

'They have that kind of technology?' Ross wanted to know.

Sandra shook her head.

'No, but money goes a long way out here. You'd be surprised what other officers would do for a spare bit of cash. One of the reasons we have such a big problem with the memory smuggling in the city is because of traffickers paying officers to transport them inside. Sometimes the dirty bastards will even use their own heads to do it.' She shuddered.

Clive pointed towards a thick wooden door.

A voice could be heard on the other side of it, as could the whispering of others.

Then, with a sudden jolt, Ross realised that he recognised the voice. It was the last man Alex had seen before he died, the man who murdered him.

'In many cases,' began the soft and soothing voice. 'A stronger personality with a longer-lasting memory can overpower the host. If a full memory transfer is completed, the two full memories will struggle for survival. That, which has the strongest will almost always wins out, suffocating the weaker mind. This may take days or years to happen, but in the end only one can last. But sometimes the greater mind does not destroy the other, it simply sleeps, lying beneath the surface of the other person until it is passed from host to host. Before the gift of memory transmission was given to us, thought was like a vast ocean which surrounded the world, like one insular Tahiti,' the voice drifted through the oaken door. 'It drowned all who tried to keep it to themselves. Can you imagine such a wretched existence?' The three soldiers positioned themselves around the door, listening. Ross poked his eye through the keyhole. Inside, he could see a circle of people surrounding one man, opening his arms to the crowd as he spoke. It was Damien, the man with whom Alex had spoken. 'Memory implants were the first technology and they will be the last. We have used it to excavate knowledge, immortalise love and elevate the senses…'

'Over there,' growled Clive. 'They still don't know we're here, time to move.'

They both nodded.

'…memory technology, like the coat-hanger, has never been improved on or built upon in any way since its inception. The powers that would ban full memory transfer forever, stunting our natural lives to a mere hundred years. But in all the centuries I have lived, I have been a father, a mother, a leader and a follower. Who amongst them can say the same? Why do they deny us the experience of relating to one another? Like in all things, we must change our society just enough so that everything can remain the same. Pure and uncorrupted.'

Clive reached inside his bag and brought out a charge, lit red and coated with sticky paste. It took him a few minutes to prime the device before planting it on the door where a knocker would usually be.

Clive held up three silent fingers.

'That is why I have decided to use it…'

One, he mouthed. A finger was lowered.

Ross felt a bead of sweat roll down his face.

'…for the reason it was first created…'

Two—another finger went down.

'…to allow us to live, as we are, forever.'

Three.

The charge blew the door apart, breaking the wood upon detonation and sending splinters flying into the faces of the men waiting on the other side. Ross dashed through behind

Clive and Sandra after the smoke cleared to reveal four startled traffickers. Ross started as he recognised a jagged facial scar on one of the men's cheeks, the same leering thug who had struck Alex from behind. All of their eyes were a furious red from the amount of positive memory they'd been uploading into their heads. One shouted something to his friend who reached under the nearest desk, grasping with a bandaged hand for something underneath.

'Show me your hands!' Ross stuck the barrel of his rifle right between the eyes of the disfigured trafficker. 'I said show me your—'

Two gunshots erupted from Sandra's rifle and the man collapsed with a pair of smoking holes in his back. The room turned into a lightning storm, all flashes and thunderclaps. The three officers pressed further into the heart of the control room, guided by their flashlights and the illuminating gunfire.

A hail of bullets forced them to duck behind cover. Ross winced as he heard them snap and pop right next to his feet and tucked them under himself in a blind panic to avoid getting hit. The rifle felt clunky and cumbersome in his sweat-drenched hands. There was a rattling sound vibrating across the room. It sounded close, echoing over the sound of shouting and gunfire. It took Ross a moment to realise that he was shaking uncontrollably and that the rattling noise was the butt of his gun knocking next to the wall he was crouched behind.

'Rookie!' Clive bellowed from behind an overturned computer desk. 'Your combat uploader, use it now.'

He could hear Clive shouting. His voice was muffled as if he were underwater.

His pouch, where was his pouch?

The whole room was shaking. The corners of his eyes had gone dark. He felt small and useless. Then, clenching his teeth, he focused, finding his combat uploader and grasping it with trembling fingers, then scrambled away from the spot he had been standing on not a moment earlier. A pistol shot blew a monitor apart in front of him. He reached inside and pulled out the shining metal tip, coated with sisyphum. He took only a second to steady himself before plunging the metal into the back of his skull.

He hit upload.

Ross waited, thinking that his heart must be about to explode from the force of its own hammering. Curses and cries rang out as wounded traffickers were dragged back by their comrades, spilling blood over keyboards and knotted wires.

Then, he noticed his heart-beat had begun to slow and his breaths had become calm and shallow while his muscles began to relax themselves.

He picked up his rifle from the ground.

Ross blinked as he held his finger down on the trigger and when he opened his eyes, he was surrounded by green fields and meadows. The meadows were on fire and the sun was blacked-out by the smoke. There were greasy, unwashed men all around him; all of them dressed in dogged grey uniforms, smattered by dirt and blood. They were standing on top of a hill and the rifle he had been carrying was now a machine gun, mounted on top of sandbags. His sergeant was bellowing at him to point it down into a valley where smoke layered the scene.

There was a whooshing noise and hot air. He looked up to the sky. Dozens of airplanes could be seen silhouetted against the morning sun and hundreds of figures wearing camouflaged gear were drifting down from the clouds. Screams could be heard amongst the sound of swooping aircraft as some of the airborne landed amidst the flaming meadows. He heard a roar down in the valley as the battle lines broke and a sea of green-coloured soldiers swarmed over the barbed wire and began to charge up the battlements towards them. His eyes feasted on the bonfire. He saw road signs in Mandarin, aflame—lands brighter than the sky above them, smothered by tar-smoke. Far below him, he saw a river where a thousand bodies floated. His eyes adjusted until he noticed the oil spill. Leaking down, the fire danced across the water, leaping over the bank to the many homes which lay waiting on the far shore. The whole river was soon ablaze and all the bodies were burning, their skin cracking like ripe marshmallows, eyeballs shrivelling in their sockets and deflating like gently-squashed grapes.

'Fire!' screamed his commander as the tide of men rolled up the hill. 'Fire!'

Ross blinked twice, shaking the memories out of his head and focusing his attention back on himself. The smell of burning flesh subsided for the moment.

Remember your training.

He closed his eyes, and when he opened them, he was back in the control room amidst another fire-fight and the half-dozen dealers who had been in front of him were now dead. He could hear Sandra cursing from up on the catwalks, still alive, and could see Clive hounding the remaining dealer and cutting off his escape. After a few minutes, the room fell into silence once again.

'Well,' said Clive, after a few moments. 'Looks like that's all of them. Nice work.'

'Rookie, how many did you take out? Three?'

'Not enough,' muttered Ross as his combat memories began to fade down to a manageable level.

'Doesn't matter,' said Clive. 'It's over now.'

'Yes,' a voice echoed around the cavern. 'It's all over now.'

All three officers whirled around, pointing their flashlights towards the corner of the room where the voice was coming from. One of the traffickers was still alive. There was a wound on his thigh and another where Ross' bullet had grazed his neck. He had propped himself upright against a rust-caked table. He gazed at them with weary black eyes; eyes that Ross recognised.

'It's him!' he shouted to the others. 'The one who killed Alex. His name's Damien.'

Clive stepped towards him, looking Damien up and down then grunting and lowering his rifle. Damien spluttered, wheezing in and out of his punctured airway with shuddering lethargy. Ross lurched forwards and grabbed hold of Damien's face, forcing him to look upwards. 'You sick creep,' he growled. 'I hope the money you got off the sisyphum made it worth killing him.'

Damien wheezed through the hole in his neck, gurgling blood.

'Us, kill him?' he giggled, making Ross turn a violent red. 'Seems like quite a feat, considering the million-dollar combat memories you lot have in your skulls.' He wheezed, gasping for air as Ross held him. 'They were glad you know.'

His eyes rolled up to meet Ross'. 'They thanked us. I took nothing and they weren't willing to give.'

Ross tightened his grip. 'You took every positive memory they had.' He pointed to the piles of empty uploaders, scattered next to the dealers. 'All for pleasure and money—that's all they were worth to you. You deserve to suffer.'

For the first time, Damien looked mournful.

'This is your first time out of the city, isn't it?' His face cracked into a bloody smile as he nodded towards the pile of empty uploaders, strewn across the control room floor. Damien grabbed hold of Ross' collar, pulling him close and whispering. 'If you wanted to stop corruption, you're in the wrong profession. People will do anything to get into the city, and there are plenty willing to look the other way to let them get there. Just ask your sergeant here. Any memory can be altered, kid, remember that.'

Clive moved forward and knocked him down again. 'Stay down,' he growled.

His eyes began to cloud over and his voice went soft.

'I've lived a thousand lives. There's nothing you can do to me that hasn't been done a hundred times over. So, go ahead, you might as well—'

Blood spurted out from between his fingers as a bullet punctured Damien's right lung, silencing him forever. 'Not worth listening to, lad' said Clive, his gun still smoking. 'People like him are liars by instinct. C'mon, we've been here long enough.'

Ross let Damien's body fall to the floor to reveal the rust-caked table he had been sitting on. He looked for the mask that he remembered from Alex's memories, along with the drill that they'd used to kill him. The table was empty.

On the wall, there was a map. The map was of a night sky and every star had been mapped and labelled, connecting every dot which could be seen from earth. Next to the star was a face, a picture of the mules who were being kept in the mine. Every star was joined to a person, dozens of people. Then there was a drawing of Damien himself.

'What will happen to the mules?' he asked Clive just as they were about to leave. The old man stopped to look at him and frowned, his forehead turning into a cobweb of creases. 'The medics are taking them back to the surface now— They'll be given new implants and new lives. We have a policy that any affected peoples are to be brought back to the cities for rehabilitation. The state will look after them now— but that's not for you to worry about, kid. You've done your job. Let's get back to civilization.'

Ross grunted and let himself be led away. He stopped to look at the body of one of the traffickers. It was the one with the scar running down the side of his face, except the man was old, frail. He looked barely able to run, let along swing a rifle. He looked for a rifle by the body and found none. When he looked up, he saw Clive stooping over Damien's body, his hand outstretched, holding something to the back of the corpse's head.

When Clive stood up before Ross hurried back to the paramedics, he could have sworn he caught a glimpse of Clive stuffing an upload uploader into his pocket.

The last thing Ross saw before he hopped on board the extraction vehicle was the eight-year-old girl being led to the medical unit, gazing with hazelnut brown eyes back at the empty mud huts littering the side of the lake. She stared past her mother who was being escorted up the ramp and into the vehicle beside her, then back to the mineshaft as though they were forgetting something down in the. caverns, something important which no one else knew about Ross watched them amble up the slope and right before the doors closed and shut them into darkness, something Damien had said echoed around his mind:

People will do anything to get into the city.

The engines reared as they set off towards the distant marble walls while the officers jolted and rocked, passing over lone and level sands that stretched far away into the distance. Ross saw the trucks loading up on the sisyphum they'd captured from the traffickers. He thought about asking Clive what was going to happen to it all, but when he glanced over to the front of the truck, he saw Clive uploading a memory. It had a silver casing, meaning it wasn't military issue. When he was finished, he switched it back into his pocket and closed the shutter behind him. Ross looked down, frowning as he pulled out the probe Sandra had given him to extract Aaron's memory at the start of the day, then lifted it towards his ear.

It was humming softly.

The Drift

They continued until they were in the middle of the pacific where they stopped and thanked the ferryman who they paid in silver for their journey. Each of their hands were stiff with age, but they nudged the sack of rocks that chafed their feet to the edge of the boat all the same, and took each other's palms before standing on the precipice. When all was ready, they dropped the rocks into the sea, then, before the chains around their ankles could pull them under, they jumped after them.

She floated down to the bottom of the sea, leaving the memories behind her. Far above, the boat she had jumped from rocked steadily atop the surface. With a sigh, she let all air pass out of her lungs and breathed in fine salt water through her nostrils to make her heavy. She sank, unable to tell up from down. The light faded as her body drifted deeper towards the ocean floor. She drifted for days, months, her heavy clothes and skin weighing her down.

Sooner than she had expected, she felt the small nibbles of fish who had come to eat her. They tore tiny chunks of her arms and legs and darted away in fear. She did not mind. Let them feed, they would not get at the metal underneath which kept her alive. So terribly alive.

She was heavier without the flesh to buoy her and she began to sink quicker as more of her body parts were nibbled away. Without warning, something plucked at her eye, leaving her half blind, then in a flash, the other was gone along with it and she sank in darkness. After a while, all of her tender meat and muscle was gone and only her metallic remains floated further towards the sea floor. She wondered momentarily if some larger creature would come and crush her bones to satisfy its own curiosity—as must have happened to so many others who had drifted before her—tugging her limbs from each other. She waited and waited. Nothing touched her. All sensation had departed, leaving only her gentle drifting.

Clunk.

She hit the ocean floor.

Stillness came like an old friend to envelope her in its embrace as what was left of her body sagged and went limp, resting itself against the stone. She felt nothing. Everything inside her was dead, save her memories. Her memories which included watching the others fly away in their many ships, leaving the rest of them on this wretched world which death had forgotten. She had stayed behind, wanting to live forever with the earth. She would never be a part of their cult, and this was her reward. What did they think they were going to find out there? Some new world where something existed that could kill them? They were long past that now. They had gotten what they all wanted and now they must suffer for it. All things had been made, all words uttered and all deeds done. It would last forever, she would last forever, useless and unforgettable.

Her mind wandered as the rest of her stubbornly refused to die. She wondered how many others were here with her, cursed with the long life, sitting alone in the darkness, their flesh long rotted away but their minds and memories intact, thinking as she was. If only there were some ways to reach them? But then there had been plenty of chances to do that on the surface, her fellows were the reason she was down here instead of up there. She enjoyed their company much more. The numbness stretched on and her thoughts with it until the dull metal began to fade.

***

The man wretched the uploader out of his head and gasped for breath, beating his fists on the salt rocks and swallowing buckets of air as he tried to stop himself from drowning.

'You're awake, you fool,' his companions shook him, bursting echoes into his head until his senses returned.

The man looked down at the metal fragments they had retrieved from the bottom of the ravine. 'What happened?' they asked him again and again and again, ringing the words into his echo locator. *What happened what happened what happened.*

'There was a great ocean,' he echoed to them. *A great ocean.*

'This woman tried to drown herself,' *drown herself.*

'The creatures here ate her but her memory survived. She was one of the ones left behind before the great torment was reversed.' *was reversed.*

They echoed back and forth to alarming speed, bouncing over the great empty cavern.

A sea? Here?

Filled with water, yes.

The rest, littered with metal bones, all rusted billions of years ago.

We should tell the others.

Find more memories.

Yes, more. More records.

Then spun to action, searching among the dry ravine for remnants of a species long extinct.

The man was pleased that he had volunteered to upload the memory of the remains. His bravery would be recorded and, in turn, perhaps even his memory would one day be precious to another, once they had left the planet of their origin, and the earth was left to crisp into a red husk as its sun decayed, drying up its oceans and bleaching its atmosphere.

He looked at the woman's remains and was happy. Her memories were still intact, and so in some ways she still existed, but they had stopped the pain which plagued so many others millions of years ago, and they could now put their ancestors to rest where they belonged—just as the first sun of their species took its last breaths.

He picked up her metal fragments and sealed the memory into the transport container. She would not be granted peace just yet, but at least she would have company.

***

They took the uploader from their collective node and placed it back amongst the others to contemplate. Much time had passed since they had thought of their own mortality, how everything they held precious only had meaning because of the threat of annihilation. It was a threat their kind had been struggling with for millennia. Now, at last, that threat was with them again.

The last suns were beginning to fade and dwarf into viscous arrays of molten dust as the gas giants smouldered among the black canvas of space. One by one, their lights went out as quickly as they had come—back from a time when they had no memory fragments from which to recall— and watched as the gaseous giants began their slumber, just as the last of humankind soon would, too.

Millions of ships landed on what their inhabitants knew would be their final resting place. There could be no more worlds, no more stars to create, and no more will to create them. They had stored what little they could, knowing that ultimately it would remain unread and unheard, as a trillion-year-old belief in extraterrestrial formations had been eradicated for good once the universe had been fully explored. There was no one to take the rains once they were gone. Still, they welcomed the newcomers with open arms, and set about making preparations for the last of the species.

***

I take the last uploader and place it back in the collection, taking care to polish it along with the others, as I have been doing since my birth. I have viewed every stored memory known to my kind. And at last, I can breathe the final breath of my species. I have lived a billion lives, loved more people than could ever exist in a single memory and destroyed, gained and lost everything which has ever existed.

I line up all the memories I have collected over the millennia; this will be my last. Memories of friends, enemies, lovers and losers. All my old memories, and all the rest I have absorbed or recovered along the way. I, who left my body long ago. I, who bought a ticket for Carriage A, who stole artefacts from a warehouse, who cleaned up after homicides, who hid from police. I, who allowed humankind to live as long as they would choose. I, who brought people and experience together, who made the first journey to the stars, who visited every single one I counted. Here, now, at the last one. I place this last memory with the others and wait for the star to eat itself. I step onto the precipice of space as the last light which will ever be starts to turn red. I stand over the Lethe, that oblivious pool, seeing the reflection of a thousand faces in its opaque waters, and ready myself for the dive.

I open the airlock and drift.